D0976946

THE BIG FIELD

MIKE LUPICA

THE BIG FIELD

Philomel Books

PHILOMEL BOOKS

A division of Penguin Young Readers Group.

Published by The Penguin Group.

Penguin Group (USA) Inc., 375 Hudson Street, New York, NY 10014, U.S.A. Penguin Group (Canada), 90 Eglinton Avenue East, Suite 700, Toronto, Ontario M4P 2Y3, Canada (a division of Pearson Penguin Canada Inc.). Penguin Books Ltd, 80 Strand, London WC2R 0RL, England. Penguin Ireland, 25 St. Stephen's Green, Dublin 2, Ireland (a division of Penguin Books Ltd). Penguin Group (Australia), 250 Camberwell Road, Camberwell, Victoria 3124, Australia (a division of Pearson Australia Group Pty Ltd). Penguin Books India Pvt Ltd, 11 Community Centre, Panchsheel Park, New Delhi - 110 017, India. Penguin Group (NZ), 67 Apollo Drive, Rosedale, North Shore 0632, New Zealand (a division of Pearson New Zealand Ltd.) Penguin Books (South Africa) (Pty) Ltd, 24 Sturdee Avenue, Rosebank, Johannesburg 2196, South Africa. Penguin Books Ltd, Registered Offices: 80 Strand, London WC2R 0RL, England.

Copyright © 2008 by Mike Lupica.

All rights reserved. This book, or parts thereof, may not be reproduced in any form without permission in writing from the publisher, Philomel Books, a division of Penguin Young Readers Group, 345 Hudson Street, New York, NY 10014. Philomel Books, Reg. U.S. Pat. & Tm. Off. The scanning, uploading and distribution of this book via the Internet or via any other means without the permission of the publisher is illegal and punishable by law. Please purchase only authorized electronic editions, and do not participate in or encourage electronic piracy of copyrighted materials. Your support of the author's rights is appreciated. The publisher does not have any control over and does not assume any responsibility for author or third-party websites or their content.

Published simultaneously in Canada.

Printed in the United States of America.

Book design by Richard Amari.

Library of Congress Cataloging-in-Publication Data

Lupica, Mike.

The big field / Mike Lupica.

p. cm.

Summary: When fourteen-year-old baseball player Hutch feels threatened by the arrival of a new teammate named Darryl, he tries to work through his insecurities about both Darryl and his remote and silent father, who was once a great ballplayer too. [1. Baseball—Fiction. 2. Fathers and sons—Fiction.] I. Title. PZ7.L97914Bi 2008 [Fic]—dc22 2007023647

ISBN 978-0-399-24625-8

1 3 5 7 9 10 8 6 4 2

ACKNOWLEDGMENTS

The great Esther Newberg, William Goldman, Susan Burden and Michael Green, the first response team as all of these books are being written. Shandel Richardson of the *South Florida Sun-Sentinel*.

And Bene and Lee Lupica: I write a lot about parents. My own parents first showed me, and continue to show me, how to get it right.

Once again for Taylor, Christopher, Alex, Zach and Hannah.

People ask all the time why I believe in happy endings. My wife and children are why.

THE BIG FIELD

IF YOU WERE A SHORTSTOP, YOU ALWAYS WANTED THE BALL HIT AT YOU.

Whether the game was on the line or not.

Keith Hutchinson, known to his friends as Hutch, had always thought of himself as the captain of any infield he'd ever been a part of, all the way back to his first year of Little League. Even back then, he could see that other kids were scared to have the ball hit at them in a big spot. Not Hutch. It was the shortstop in him. If the ball was in play, he always wanted it to be *his* play.

Especially now.

Because the game was on the line now.

And it wasn't just any old game; it was the biggest of the summer so far.

Hutch's American Legion team, the Boynton Beach Post 226 Cardinals, still had the lead against the Palm Beach Post 12 Braves in the finals of their 17-and-under league, even though this year's Cardinals didn't have a single 17–year-old on the team. But their lead was down to a single run now, 7–6. They were in the bottom of the ninth at the Santaluces Athletic Complex in Lantana, bases loaded for the Braves. One out to go.

If the Cardinals got the out and won the game, they moved on to the South Florida regionals next weekend, one round closer to the state finals.

If they lost, they went home.

Hutch walked over and stood behind second base, almost on the outfield grass, and waited there while their coach, Mr. Cullen, talked things over on the mound with Paul Garner, whom Mr. Cullen had just brought in to pitch.

Hutch knew what everybody on their team knew, that Paul was going to be the last Cardinals pitcher of the night, win or lose. He was going to get an out here and their season would continue, or the Braves' cleanup hitter, Billy Ray Manning, known as Man-Up Manning, was going to hit one hard someplace and it would be the Braves who'd be playing the next round.

Hutch and his teammates would be done for the summer. Done like dinner.

No more baseball, just like that.

He didn't even want to think about it.

Paul was one of his favorite guys on the team, normally their starting left fielder, but he was only the fourth best pitcher they had. Yet Mr. Cullen had been forced to pull their closer, Pedro Mota, after Pedro had suddenly forgotten how to pitch with two outs and nobody on and the Cardinals still ahead, 7–4. First he'd given up three straight hits to load the bases. He'd wild-pitched one run home after that, before walking the next hitter to reload the bases. Finally, he hit the next batter and just like that, it was 7–6, and Mr. Cullen had seen enough.

Now the one guy in the world they didn't want to see at the plate, Man-Up Manning—a seventeen-year-old lefty who actually did look like a man to Hutch—was standing next to the plate, waiting to get his swings.

No place to put him. No way to pitch around him.

Paul didn't throw hard, but he threw strikes, kept the ball down, got a lot of ground balls when he was pitching at his best.

One stinking ground ball now and they were in the regionals.

More important, they got to keep playing.

Hit it to me, he thought.

Mr. Cullen patted Paul on the shoulder, left him to throw his warm-up pitches. Hutch thought about going over to talk to Darryl Williams while he did. But they never talked much during the game, not even during pitching changes. When they did, it was usually only about which one of them would cover second if they thought a guy might be stealing.

Nobody was stealing now. Hutch wasn't paying much attention to the guy on first. Nobody was. He was a lot more worried about the runners on second and third, the potential tying and winning runs. Darryl? As usual, he didn't look worried about anything. He was staring off, lost in his own thoughts or lost in space. Darryl never seemed to look tense or worried or anxious. He knew he was the best hitter on their team—the best player, period. And yet . . .

And yet baseball seemed to bore him sometimes.

Paul threw his last warm-up pitch. Brett Connors, their

catcher, came out to have one quick word with him. As he ran back, the neighborhood people sitting on the other side of the screen behind home plate began to applaud, understanding the importance of the moment, as if they were all suddenly sensing the magic of what baseball could do to a summer's night.

Hutch watched them and thought: If we lose, some of these same people will be here tomorrow night watching the older kids play the 19-and-under game. Their season wouldn't end. Mine would.

Hit it to me.

He walked away from the bag, got into his ready position, watched Brett go through a bunch of signals behind the plate, all of which Hutch knew were totally bogus. Paul had one pitch: A dinky fastball with a late break to it that guys usually couldn't lay off of, even on balls that were about to end up in the dirt.

Paul threw one in the dirt now, but Man-Up Manning didn't bite.

Ball one.

"Be patient!" the Braves coach yelled from their bench. "He's trying to make you chase."

Paul threw a strike that Man-Up was taking all the way, then missed just outside.

Two-and-one.

"Still a hitter's count," the Braves coach said.

Is it ever, Hutch thought.

He could feel his heart in his chest, feeling the thump-

thump-thump of it the way you could feel the thump of rap music from the car next to you at a stoplight sometimes.

Knowing that this was when he loved playing baseball so much, he thought his heart might actually *explode.* He loved it all the time, Hutch knew, loved it more than anybody he knew, on this team or any team he'd ever played on, loved the history of it, loved the stats and the numbers and the way they connected the old days to right now.

Most of all Hutch loved it when you were playing to keep playing, when you were at the plate the way Man-Up was, or standing in the middle of a diamond like this and hoping—begging—for the ground ball that would get you and your teammates the heck out of here with a win.

Paul Garner took a deep breath to settle himself, let it out, shook his pitching hand before he got back on the rubber. Because of the way Paul snapped his wrist, his ball broke more like a screwball, which meant *away* from lefties.

He threw his very best pitch now, on the outside corner, at the knees, right where Brett Connors had set his glove.

And as mighty a swing as Man-Up tried to put on the ball, swinging for the fences all the way, going for the grand slam hero swing, the best he could do was get the end of his bat on it. It would have been a weak grounder for anybody else. But Man-Up truly was a beast, even when he got beat on a pitch this way.

He hit it hard the other way, toward the shortstop hole, between second and third.

Instinctively, as soon as he saw the ball come off the end of the bat, Hutch was moving to his right, knowing that the only chance they were going to have, if the ball didn't end up in left field, was a force at second.

The shortstop in Hutch processed all that in an instant.

Only he wasn't the shortstop.

Darryl was.

HUTCH WAS PLAYING SECOND, MOVING TO HIS RIGHT TO COVER
the base, watching from there as Darryl was in the hole in
a blink, moving faster than anybody else on the field when
he had to, backhanding the ball, already starting to turn his
body as he did, gloving the ball cleanly and transferring it
to his right hand, snapping off a throw from his hip without
even looking to see where it was going.

Do-or-die.

Make the play and the Cardinals win.

Throw it away and the other guys do.

The throw was on the money, as Hutch knew it would be.

The break they got, one they sure needed, was that it was
the Braves catcher running from first. Slowest guy on their
team. So he did matter after all. Maybe if the Braves coach
had known how much it was going to matter, he would have
sent in a pinch runner. But he hadn't. He was only worried
about the tying and winning runs the way everybody else was
under the lights at Santaluces.

Hutch stretched like a first baseman now, stretched as
far as he could while still keeping his foot on the bag, his left
arm out as far as it could go. . . .

Willing Darryl's throw to get there in time.

The shortstop in him still wanting the ball as much as he ever had.

Then it was in the pocket of his glove, the worn-in pocket of his Derek Jeter model, a split second before he felt the Braves catcher hit second base, heard that sweet pop in his mitt right before he heard an even sweeter sound from the field ump behind him:

"Out!"

Game over.

Cardinals 7, Braves 6.

They were going to the regionals.

Even if somebody else had gone into the hole.

● ● ●

"The golden boy makes one play," Cody Hester was saying, "and people act like he won the game all by himself."

Cody was the Cardinals right fielder, and Hutch's best friend in the world.

"The play *was* kind of golden," Hutch said. "Even you have to admit that."

Cody grinned. "Yeah, it was." He was finished with his milk shake, but made one last slurpy sound with his straw, just for Hutch's benefit. "I'm still not sure he's the greatest teammate in the world."

"When you're a great player, there's no rule that says you have to be," Hutch said.

Cody said, "Seriously, though. You don't think the guy's

a little too full of himself? He acts like he's better than everybody else."

"Only because he is better than everybody else." Now he grinned. "And I don't think he goes around big-timing anybody. He's just cool is all."

They were sitting on the steps in front of Hutch's house in East Boynton, finishing the milk shakes they'd stopped for on the way home from the game. Cody's dad, who worked for the phone company, had dropped them at the Dairy Queen on Seacrest and told them they could walk the rest of the way if they promised to go straight to Hutch's, which they had.

Hutch and his mom and dad lived here on Gateway, in a house faded to the color of lemon-lime Gatorade that his parents talked about painting every year and yet never did. Cody's house was right around the corner on Seacrest, not even a five-minute walk away. His family had moved down to Palm Beach County from Pensacola when Cody was five, and he and Hutch had been more like brothers than friends ever since. They didn't just have a lot in common, they pretty much had everything in common, starting with baseball. They didn't go through life worrying about how neither one of their families had a lot of money. Or that they lived in the neighborhood that they did. Or that Cody's house—a shade of pink that Cody liked to say even flamingos would find gross—was an even uglier color than Hutch's.

As long as they had each other, and a game to play, they thought things were pretty solid.

Now they had more games to play. First the regionals. If they got through that, they played for the state championship on the big field at Roger Dean Stadium in Jupiter, where the real Cardinals and the Marlins played their spring training games. Not only did they play at Roger Dean, they got to play on television, since this was the first year that the Sun Sports Network would be broadcasting the Legion finals, in all age groups, the way ESPN televised the Little League World Series.

Hutch knew it would be a cool thing to make it up the road to Roger Dean, maybe get the chance to play on television for the first time in his life.

Yet what mattered most to Hutch was that they were still playing, that they'd gotten out of the bottom of the ninth tonight with their season still intact.

Out of the blue, Cody said, "This is going to be the greatest summer ever!"

"You say that every summer."

"This time I really mean it," Cody said. "And you know I mean it because it isn't the summer we were *supposed* to have."

Hutch knew what he meant. That was the best thing about having a best friend—having a conversation and being able to leave stuff out.

What Cody had meant was this:

When they used to talk about winning the state championship of Legion ball, even before they were old enough to play Legion ball, it was supposed to happen with Hutch playing short and Cody playing second. The way things had always been.

Then Darryl Williams had come along. Now he was at

short and Hutch had moved over to second, forcing Cody to move to right.

Darryl Williams was already treated like he was the LeBron James of baseball, a kid who was supposed to be the best shortstop—no, the best *player*—to come out of the state since Alex Rodriguez came out of Miami.

He was the same age as Hutch and Cody, fourteen, eighth grade going into ninth. He lived in Lantana, and had played on a Lantana Babe Ruth team during the school year. But summers were for Legion ball and the best Lantana kids played for Post 226, same as the best Boynton Beach kids did. There had been some talk that Darryl, even at fourteen, was good enough to play up to the 19-and-under team from Post 226. But once Darryl showed up for tryouts, making it official that he'd decided to play for the Cardinals—maybe putting off facing nineteen-year-old pitchers for one more year—Hutch knew he would have to switch positions. It was just a question of whether it would be to another infield position or to the outfield.

This wasn't like when A-Rod got traded to the Yankees, and he knew before he even got there that shortstop belonged to Jeter. Hutch was new to the Cardinals the way the rest of the kids were, so it wasn't like this was his team the way the Yankees were Jeter's team. Hutch was moving and there wasn't anything he could say or do to change that. Once Mr. Cullen picked the whole team, he decided to move Hutch to second and put Hank Harding, an ex-catcher, at third.

So Hutch moved over from short, Cody moved from

second to right, and that was their team, the youngest ever trying to win the state championship at this age level. No 17-year-olds—just two 16-year-olds, Paul Garner and their ace, Tripp Lyons. And more 14-year-olds than 15-year-olds.

Now "Cullen's Kids," as Hutch's mom called them sometimes, were one step closer to the title, having made it to the second round.

"You know what the real bottom line is with Darryl?" Hutch said. "He's the best player we've ever played with or against, and if you love baseball the way we do, you gotta love watching him play ball."

"I'd tell you I agree with you," Cody said, "but then I'd have to kill you."

"Darryl's the reason it doesn't kill *me* that I'm not playing short," Hutch said. "It'd be like a golfer getting bent out of shape that he has to play number two behind Tiger."

Cody stood up now, walked up the sidewalk and opened the gate to the chain-link fence in front of the Hutchinsons' house, one of the few two-story houses in the whole neighborhood, even if it looked like one of the oldest. Hutch had never given much thought to that fence, just because it had always been there, and was like a lot of the other front-yard fences in their neighborhood. It was Cody who made a big deal of it, saying that some people grew up in white-picket-fence neighborhoods, and other people grew up with fences like theirs.

"I'm gonna say it one last time," Cody said. "You won the game tonight, not him."

"Yeah, yeah," Hutch said.

Hutch watched him until he disappeared around the corner, thinking about what Cody had said about the game.

Yeah, he told himself. I did get those three hits tonight. I did drive in four runs. I *did* make a play in the fourth, going into short right, that saved a couple of runs.

But anybody who watched the game was going to remember the play Darryl had made in the ninth.

On *my* ball, Hutch thought.

He was never going to admit that out loud, not even to his best friend, but there it was. In his heart Hutch knew he would get over not playing short on a date Cody liked to call the twelfth of never.

• • •

He went up to his room and turned on the small fan he had on his desk. The heat was always brutal in Florida in the summer, but the past few days had been even hotter and muggier than usual, and even the thunderstorm that had blown through the area about an hour before the game tonight hadn't done anything to cool things off. There were only two rooms in their house that had air-conditioning: the living room and his parents' bedroom. But his parents were down in the living room watching a movie they'd rented from Blockbuster, and so Hutch had come up here to listen to the Marlins-Mets game on the radio.

He stripped down to his shorts, trained the fan at the head of his bed, lay down on sheets that wouldn't feel cool for long, and tried to concentrate on the Marlins.

Problem was, there were shortstops all around him. The poster of his hero, Jeter, over his bed and the one of Cal Ripken Jr. over his desk. On the ceiling was Ozzie Smith, "the Wizard of Oz," doing that backflip he used to do when he ran out to play short for the Cardinals.

Not to mention the best shortstop in the house, the one downstairs watching the movie:

His dad.

He had been the first Hutch Hutchinson, even if he no longer went by that nickname. He was just back to being plain old Carl Hutchinson. He'd told Hutch he was going to try to make the game tonight, but he never showed. Again. This time, he said, it was because one of the other drivers hadn't shown up at the driving service he worked for, and he'd had to make an airport run to Miami.

His dad always seemed to have a good reason when he missed a game.

Sometimes Hutch thought it was because he just didn't love baseball anymore, because baseball had broken his heart, because he was supposed to be on his way to the big leagues once and never made it out of East Boynton.

It's not going to happen that way with me, Hutch told himself now.

Even if I am playing second base—more like second fiddle, actually—to Darryl.

It's only for a couple of months, he kept telling himself. Cody liked to say that none of this was going to matter when they got to Boynton Beach High and Darryl was playing for

Santaluces Community and Hutch was back at his normal position.

But Cody didn't know something, even though he thought he knew *everything* about Hutch. Cody Hester didn't know, at least not yet, about Hutch's dream of getting out of East Boynton, getting out of Florida and playing his high school baseball a long way from here, on a baseball scholarship at one of the fancy boarding schools up north in New Jersey he'd been reading about. One of the schools with famous baseball programs to go along with their basketball programs.

Baseball was going to be his ticket out of here even if it hadn't been his dad's.

And Hutch believed in his heart that his best chance to do that was at short. If you followed baseball the way he did, and nobody he knew followed baseball the way he did, you knew that a great shortstop was worth his weight in gold.

Just look around: The Yankees had Jeter and the Rangers had Michael Young and the Mets had José Reyes, whom Hutch just liked watching *run* more than anybody else in baseball, playing any position. The Marlins had Manny Ramírez's brother Hanley, and even the little guy who played short for the St. Louis Cardinals, David Eckstein, had ended up the MVP of the World Series a couple of years ago.

On the radio now, above the noise from the fan, he heard one of the Marlins' announcers, Dave Van Horne, his voice excited, the words jumping across the room, talking about Hanley Ramírez moving to his left and snapping off a throw to first to beat the runner by a step.

"What can I tell you, folks," Van Horne yelled, "the kid's a star!"

Why not? Hutch thought. Hanley's playing a star position. You had to know that whether you were a team guy or not.

The scouts didn't come to see second basemen.

DARRYL WAS LATE FOR PRACTICE MONDAY AFTERNOON.

It wasn't the first time.

He hadn't been late for a game yet, even though there'd been some pretty close calls, including the championship game last Friday night. He'd shown up fifteen minutes before the first pitch, after the rest of the team had taken both batting practice and infield.

Today, he said, he thought he was getting a ride from a friend of his mom's, but the friend had never shown up.

So he had to go take the bus to Caloosa instead.

Which was late.

"Coach," he said, smiling in an embarrassed way, "I'm sorry this sounds like such a lame excuse, but it's the truth."

"Relax, Darryl," Mr. Cullen said, not even looking up from the end of the bench, where he was making out the order for batting practice. "I believe you."

"Even so," Darryl said.

"Even so, nothing," Mr. Cullen said. "It's the same off the field as it is on: You can only control what you can control."

"You're the man, Mr. C," Darryl said.

Darryl must have sprinted from the bus stop and across the Little League field at Caloosa Park, where they were practicing today, because he was acting as if he was out of breath, like he was standing on third base after hitting a triple.

"Now go get yourself a drink of water and get ready to hit while I get warmed up," Mr. Cullen said. "You can go third, after Cody and Hutch."

Mr. Cullen usually liked to pitch BP rather than waste somebody's arm or put somebody on the mound who couldn't get the ball over the plate and would just aggravate the hitters. He went out to the mound now and threw some warm-up pitches to Brett Connors while Cody and Hutch waited near the on-deck circle at Caloosa.

"You think I'd be hitting third if I showed up right before BP?" Cody said when Darryl was out of earshot.

"What I think," Hutch said, "is that you should shut up and hit."

Cody walked away, shaking his head, saying, "I can't believe people think you're the nice one."

Hutch leaned on his bat as he watched Mr. Cullen pitch to Cody, who had an open stance and was a dead pull hitter, legendary for scattering guys on the third-base side of the field with screaming foul balls when he'd open up his hips too early. Hutch was actually less interested in Cody's batting style than in seeing how hard Mr. Cullen was throwing today. When he was a kid, he'd been a high school pitching star up in Vero Beach known as King Cullen. And had, he'd informed them, pitched a couple of years in the Red Sox farm system. But he hadn't thrown hard enough to become a real prospect—"Unfortunately, I was an eighties guy," he told them, "and not because I grew up in the eighties"—and had moved down to Palm Beach County to start what was now a big real estate company, even doing his own television commercials for it, which made him sort of a local celebrity.

Even though he was in his forties now, he could still throw harder than anybody in their age group. And sometimes he liked to really bring it in BP. His theory was: If his guys could hit him, they could hit anybody in Legion ball.

Hutch saw right away that he really planned to bring it today, just off his first few pitches to Cody.

"Look at him," Darryl said. "Man's sweating already like he's on the free throw line with a minute to go."

"This is gonna be one of those days when he goes out of his way to make us look bad," Hutch said.

"Not me," Darryl said.

"You sure?" Hutch made sure Darryl saw him smiling, so it didn't come across as some kind of challenge.

"Wait and see," Darryl said. "He can hump it up there as much as he wants. All's I see when I hit against him are mattress balls."

"What's a mattress ball?" Hutch said. He knew a lot of baseball expressions, and knew by now that Darryl had his own way of talking. But he'd never heard that one before.

Darryl grinned at him and said, "A pitch I can lay all over, homes."

Darryl called most guys on the team "homes." For *home-*

boys. Hutch wasn't sure if it was because Darryl just liked the expression, the cool way it sounded, or because he still didn't know everybody's names.

"Mind if I cut the line?" Darryl said now.

And, just like that, Darryl was walking casually toward home plate as Cody ran out the last ball he'd hit, acting as if deciding to change the order this way was the most natural thing in the world.

To him, maybe it is, Hutch thought.

Mr. Cullen didn't seem to notice that they were hitting out of order. Or maybe he just didn't care, because it was Darryl.

Mr. Cullen threw him a breaking ball in the dirt, grinning as he did, like he was messing with him.

The second pitch was the one. A mattress ball.

There was a tall outfield fence in Caloosa, out beyond the grass that seemed to be freshly cut here the way the infield always seemed to be freshly raked, but Hutch had only seen high school varsity players clear it.

Until now.

Darryl hit it so far over the center-field fence, one that included an ad for Ken Cullen Real Estate, that Hutch wondered if it might roll all the way to I-95.

That wasn't the most amazing thing.

The most amazing thing was that it didn't even look as if Darryl Williams had swung hard, that he'd hit a ball that hard with just a flick of his wrists.

He was already walking away from home plate while the ball was in the air, as if that was all the batting practice he needed today.

Mr. Cullen still had his back to home plate, watching the flight of the ball.

To no one in particular, he finally said, "And that, gentlemen, is why the old coach ended up in real estate instead of at Fenway Park."

Hutch stopped watching Mr. Cullen then and checked out Darryl. Thinking there had to be some reaction after you hit a baseball like that.

And there was.

Darryl was smiling, shrugging his shoulders and putting his hands out, the way Michael Jordan once did on his way to scoring thirty-five points in the first half of a game in the NBA Finals.

Like even he couldn't explain why he was this good.

• • •

Mr. Cullen had told them when the team had first been selected that they weren't going to choose a team captain until they'd gotten to know each other a little bit; if they named a captain before they even got out of the county tournament, it would be like electing a class president the first week of school.

They were sitting in a circle in the outfield the way they usually did after every practice, chugging down Gatorade and power drinks and ice water, when he announced they were going to name the captain before they went home today.

"I know you probably think it's kind of an honorary thing," he said. "And maybe you even think we don't need one on this team, because we've got a bunch of hard-working guys with great work ethics.

"But I've always thought being a team captain in sports meant something. And on every Legion team I've ever coached, going all the way back, I've always thought of my captain as being more like a player-coach."

He stood up. "Any questions?"

Brett Connors raised a hand.

"I've got one, Coach," he said. "How do you want us to do this? Should we pick a couple of names and then vote on those?"

Mr. Cullen put his hands up and walked between Hutch and Cody to the back of the circle. "You guys decide. This is your deal all the way."

Hutch actually thought Brett would make a good captain. He had grown up in Lantana before moving to East Boynton, so he had played Little League with guys from both places. He was a catcher in baseball and a middle linebacker in football, and everybody on the Cardinals knew by now, after just the handful of tournament games they'd played, that trying to get to home plate when he was blocking it was like trying to get a yard against him in football.

Every minute he was on the field, whether he was hitting or catching or just running their infield drills from the plate, he was all business. It made him Hutch's kind of ballplayer.

"Okay, then," Brett said. "I'll get this party started. I nominate Hutch to be captain."

Right away, Cody said, "Second."

Brett looked around. "Okay, we got ourselves one nomi-
nee. Any others?"

Nobody in the circle said anything. Hutch kept his head
down. He was happy that Brett thought enough of him to
think he'd make a good captain. Hutch just didn't want his
teammates to *see* him happy.

Didn't want to act as if he wanted it too much.

"Okay, let's do it another way," Brett said. "Anybody *opposed* to Hutch being captain?"

Hutch said, "I was actually going to nominate you,
Brett."

"Don't even think about it," Brett said. "Everybody knows
you should be the captain." He stood up. "Everybody for
Hutch Hutchinson, put your arm in the air."

Hutch allowed himself to look around now, and saw his
teammates' arms shooting up in the air.

Cody put both of his up.

The only one who didn't, Hutch noticed, was Darryl, who
was sitting next to Mr. Cullen in the back of the circle.

"Then Hutch it is," Brett said.

Then they were all saying "Hutch . . . Hutch . . . Hutch" as
if woofing out his nickname, and Cody was pulling Hutch to
his feet, the Cardinals all around him, trying to join hands
above his head, a bunch of guys who'd only come together
after the school year ended feeling like a team that had been
together, really together, for much longer.

It was when they broke free that Hutch noticed Darryl
walking alone toward the bench on the first-base side of
Caloosa.

When he got to the bench, he turned around, no expression on his face, put his hands on his hips, and stared directly at Hutch.

Or through him, maybe.

Then he kept walking, toward the parking lot.

It was as if a guy who didn't seem to care about anybody on the team suddenly cared about this:

Being captain of the team.

HIS DAD, HUTCH KNEW, HAD HELD A LOT OF JOBS IN HIS LIFE, even if he hadn't held on to any of them for very long.

Carl Hutchinson didn't talk much about that because he didn't talk much about anything, not for more than a few sentences at a time. Most of what Hutch knew about the different things his dad had done since he stopped playing baseball came from his mom, who had been his dad's high school sweetheart and pretty much been with him ever since.

His mom, Connie Hutchinson, the former Consuela Valentin, was born in Ponce, Puerto Rico. If Hutch had gotten the baseball in him from his dad, he had inherited his dark skin and dark eyes from his mother, who had moved to East Boynton from Puerto Rico when she was ten.

"Your father and I have been together through thick and thin," she'd say. "Sometimes extra thick on the thin."

Then she would smile and say, *"¡Ay, bendito!"* It was her catchall phrase from what she called her Spanglish, sometimes happy, sometimes sad, sometimes in between.

Carl Hutchinson had made it out of Legion ball and high school ball to the minor leagues, first in the Braves' farm system and then in the Twins'. He'd finally made it to Triple-A with the Twins, but that was as far as he made it. He was out of professional ball by the time he was twenty-four.

Carl Hutchinson tried selling cars for a while after that, because he'd always been good with cars. When that didn't work out, he started up a landscaping business with one of his old teammates from Boynton Beach High, figuring he could cash in, get a lot of business, just from people in the immediate area who remembered the kind of star ball-player he had been. He'd been a local celebrity even before his time in the minors, when he'd taken the East Boynton Little League team all the way to Williamsport, Pennsylvania, for the Little League World Series, where they'd lost in the finals to Taiwan.

His mom had told him all about that, and Hutch had watched the game on videocassette plenty of times, because his dad's year in Williamsport was one of the first years ABC had put the finals on television. Nobody else on East Boynton could do much against the Taiwan starting pitcher that day, but his dad had managed to get three hits off the kid, one of them a long home run.

The announcers had said you could never call anybody in sports a sure thing, but this East Boynton kid sure looked like one to them. They even joked that Cal Ripken Jr. would be looking over his shoulder someday, because this tall, skinny kid his teammates called Hutch was destined for shortstop in the Major Leagues.

Only, by the time he was supposed to be gaining on Cal Ripken, Carl Hutchinson was back in East Boynton, trying to sell cars.

He worked briefly as an assistant manager in his uncle's hardware store up in Juno Beach, but that didn't last, either. Nothing did.

Maybe that was why two summers ago Hutch's dad, between jobs again—needing what he always called a J-O-B— had even run the snack truck at Santaluces for a while. Hutch knew why he was doing it, because he needed the work, but every time Hutch would look over at the truck, it would feel like somebody just punched him in the stomach. Even now Hutch would look over at that truck during a break in the game and remember what it was like when he knew his dad was inside, or when he'd see his dad leaning against the side of the truck and watching from there while Hutch's team played.

Then, and now, Hutch wondered what his dad was thinking, watching his son play on one of the fields where he'd been the biggest star in the area once, the kind of star Darryl Williams was now.

Watching with those sad-looking eyes of his.

Carl Hutchinson would never come right out and say it, but Hutch knew something as well as he knew all the baseball numbers he carried around inside him:

The only job his dad ever cared about was baseball.

And it was baseball that broke his heart for good by telling him he wasn't good enough and sending him home.

• • •

Carl Hutchinson had worked with Hutch at the very beginning on baseball, the first year his son had been old enough to play tee ball. He showed him how to hold the bat and played catch with him in the yard, backing up a little bit at a time as Hutch's arm began to get stronger. Hutch had hoped that his dad, because he'd been as good as he was at baseball, might coach him in Little League someday. But he never had.

By the time Hutch was eight, he felt like he was his own coach, even on all the summer nights when he would be out behind the house in their small yard, throwing balls against the pitchback his mom had bought for him, fielding one ground ball after another until it got too dark.

There wasn't a single night he did it when he didn't keep waiting for the back door to open and his dad to come walking out, wanting to play.

It never happened.

Sometimes Hutch would look up and see his dad's face in the kitchen window, watching him. Hutch would wave. His father would wave back.

The next time he'd sneak a look over there, his dad would always be gone.

It was almost the same way with watching games on television. He could remember sitting next to his dad on the couch, his dad pointing out things about where the fielders were playing, the way a shortstop would come across the bag on a double play, somehow knowing which pitches would be the best ones to hit before the pitcher would even deliver the ball to the plate.

A guy he'd started out in the minor leagues with, a catcher named Tom McCain—now a backup with the Marlins—was still a big star with the Braves when Hutch was younger, and Carl Hutchinson would talk about the old days and what they were both like when they were kids starting out.

Over time, though, his dad began watching games, when he still watched games, by himself. Always with a can of beer next to him. It was the only time Hutch ever saw his dad drinking beer, when a game was on. Sometimes Hutch would come into the room and the game would be on with the sound turned off, almost like his dad didn't care what the announcers were saying, and he'd feel as if there were some kind of force field around his dad.

Or there should have been a sign near the door to the living room reading No Visitors Allowed.

Not even your own son.

His dad wouldn't sit through the whole game. Hutch never knew where he went, but he'd hear the door close and know his father had left again.

He came to Hutch's games when he could, even though it was never as many as Hutch wanted. It killed him when he would do something great in a game, something that in his own mind measured up to the kind of things his dad did all the time when he was Hutch's age, and he'd look up to the stands to find his mom watching, not his dad.

He'd come home after the game and try to tell his dad what had happened, describe it the best he could, explain what he was thinking and feeling when he'd made a play in the field or driven a ball somewhere to win a game, and he'd see his dad trying to act interested.

But more and more it was just that: an act.

His dad claimed he was tired. He was working two jobs now, caddying during the day at the Emerald Dunes Golf Club in West Palm, then driving for Sun Coast limousines three or four nights a week, sometimes more. But Hutch knew it wasn't just work that made his dad seem so tired all the time, so beaten, even so much older than he really was. It was more than that, something Hutch wasn't sure he understood totally or could have explained to someone:

But both of his dad's jobs involved being a caddy, really. He either carried guys around in his car, or carried their golf bags. Hutch wouldn't have admitted it, but he was embarrassed for his dad, thinking of him like some sort of *Caddyshack* caddy in his white overalls. The great ballplayer.

Maybe his dad sensed that from Hutch.

Maybe that was why the distance between them seemed to be growing all the time.

Most of the time Hutch felt as if his dad wasn't really there, as if nothing had changed since Hutch was little, when he was playing in the yard and his dad was inside the house, one minute there, the next minute gone.

THERE WERE EIGHT TEAMS IN THEIR REGIONAL, THE BOTTOM HALF of the brackets in the new version of the state American Legion tournament.

Their county, Palm Beach, was broken up into two leagues, National and American. The Cardinals had won the National League and the Tequesta Post 271 Angels had won the American. The rest of their bracket was filled up with two teams each from Dade County, Broward, and Lee/Collier, on the west coast of Florida.

It was pretty simple the rest of the way for everybody in the South regional:

Win three more games and you got to play in the World Series from their age group, against the 17-under team that won the North.

After that it was a best-of-three series at Roger Dean, every game under the lights, every game on TV for as long as it lasted.

Their version of the World Series, winner take all.

"We could be five games from winning this whole thing, you know that, right?" Cody Hester was saying.

They were sitting at a bench near the snack truck at

Santaluces, waiting to play their first game in the regionals, against a team from Naples, the Yankees.

"Or," Hutch said, ripping open a pack of gum, "we could be one loss away from your only exercise being mowing lawns the rest of the summer."

"And you are telling me this *because* . . . ?"

"Because I don't want you to think about the whole rest of the tournament," Hutch said. "I'd sort of just like you to play these suckers one at a time."

"Captain Hutchinson of the Cardinals," Cody said in a deep announcer voice, "has stressed that his team *must* take these games one at a time. As opposed to playing the games two or three at a time." Cody shook his head. "When did you turn into a football coach?"

"I didn't."

"What, you just play one on TV?"

"You know the only game I've ever cared about is the one we're getting ready to play," Hutch said.

"I know, I know," Cody said. "I just want to get to that big field at Roger Dean *so* bad."

"Where's that?" Hutch said. "The only field I can see is the one right in front of us."

It had turned out to be a home game for the Cardinals because of a flip of the coin. After this, the regionals would play themselves out down in Fort Lauderdale.

Hutch's parents and Cody's parents were all coming to the game. Hutch's dad had caddied earlier in the day and had the night off from the car service, where he had been mostly working nights since he started with them. So this would be the first game he'd seen since the Cardinals had started the county tournament.

Before Hutch's mom had driven him and Cody to Santaluces, Hutch had gone into the living room and grinned as he asked his dad, "Any last-minute advice?"

His dad was watching the ESPN show where the sportswriters bickered and kept score over who bickered the best.

"Don't try to do too much," he said to Hutch.

"Got it."

"Play within yourself," his dad said.

Same stuff he always said.

"And," his dad said, "don't try to pull everything, even if it's a lefty pitching. You're better off hitting to right."

That was it.

"See you over there," his dad said, then smiled, not at Hutch but at the television, where the host had muted one of the sportswriters. "I love it when they do that," he said.

Hutch had left him there, the air conditioner attached to the window sounding louder than a dishwasher. His mom and Cody were waiting in the car. Before Hutch walked out the front door he leaned against it, closed his eyes, and wished he could have spent just one day with his dad when his dad was young.

Wished he could have met the dad who loved baseball the way his mom said he did.

Now he and Cody walked all the way to where their bench was on the field closest to the small lake at Santaluces. Field No. 2. Their bench was over on the first-base side, the home side of Santaluces. Behind the batting screen, the neighbor-hood people were already setting up their lawn chairs, like the area was their own personal luxury suite.

"Hel-*lo*?" Cody said now.

Sometimes Cody was like background noise to Hutch, like keeping a ball game on the radio when you were reading.

"What?" Hutch said.

"You zoned out on me there for a second."

"I was just thinking about some stuff my dad told me before we left the house."

"Such as?"

Hutch smiled, then gave his head a good hard shake, as if trying to clear away any bad thoughts. Because the prospect of getting to play a game like this, maybe keep playing games like this, was too much of a happy-making thing to let any bad thoughts get in the way.

"He told me to catch anything I could in front of my right fielder," Hutch said. "Says the guy out there has the range of one of those palm trees behind the outfield walls."

Cody just looked at him, his face like a blank wall.

"Do me a favor?"

"Whatever you need."

"Don't try to be funny," Cody said. "I'm the funny one."

Hutch grabbed a ball and they started soft-tossing be-tween the bench and the first-base line. Darryl joined them. So did Brett Connors. The pregame chatter all around them began to get louder, before they were even on the field for infield, or batting practice. The guys on the Cardinals kept stealing looks across the diamond, checking out the Naples players, listening to the chatter from over there.

Hutch thought to himself: The only time in baseball that's better than the game is this.

It didn't matter what field they were using, whether it was here or at Caloosa or any of the other ballparks in Palm Beach County. Or Roger Dean, if they made it that far.

In moments like this, Hutch felt more at home here than he did at home.

Naples jumped on the Cardinals' ace, Tripp Lyons, for four
runs in the top of the first.

Before anybody was out.

Single.

Triple.

Double.

Home run.

The game had only started about five minutes ago, and
Hutch realized that the other team had already hit for the
cycle. The Naples team called itself the Yankees, even wore
Yankees pinstripes. Now they had come out swinging like
they were the *real* Yankees.

So the Cardinals were in a 4–0 hole, just like that. And it
would have gotten much worse a few minutes later without
Hutch.

Tripp had finally managed to get two outs by then. But
the other guys were threatening again, with runners on second and third. The runner on second, the Yankees catcher,
had just ripped a shot past Hank Harding at third, the ball
looking as if it were going to roll all the way into the corner
before Paul Garner cut it off. Paul then made a perfect cutoff

throw to Darryl and the Naples third-base coach held the other runner there, even though there were two outs and sometimes you took a chance in that situation, tried to steal another run on a bad throw to the plate.

Naples was down to the ninth spot in the batting order. Mr. Cullen liked to call it a soft spot for the pitcher to land, even when the pitcher was in the kind of jam Tripp was still in. Because another hit here and the score was going to be 6–0 before the Cardinals even came to the plate.

And the No. 9 hitter wasn't going to be soft.

Hutch could see it just by the way he dug in, the way he held his bat. Hutch *knew.* He hadn't paid really close attention when the Yankees were out there for fielding practice, so he wasn't sure what position this guy played. But he was a player. For one thing, he wasn't all twitchy, like a lot of hitters were once they got into the box. They were the ones who kept fooling with their batting gloves the way their heroes did on TV, the ones who had to check to see if their feet were in the exact spot they wanted.

The kind who could make baseball feel slower than a traffic jam sometimes.

This kid was up there to hit.

The first pitch was outside.

Never moved.

The next one from Tripp was a fastball right down Route 1 and the hitter was all over it, driving the ball up the middle, right between Tripp's legs before he could get his glove down, the ball looking for all the world as if it were on its way into center field.

Hutch was moving to his right as soon as the ball came off the bat. He was still learning about angles from the other side of second base, after a whole lifetime of watching the ball come off the bat from short. But he was getting better at it, more confident, every day.

He didn't fade toward the outfield grass, knowing his only chance was to cut the ball off right there if he was going to have any kind of play at first.

Hutch still had to dive at the last second, full out, and try to backhand the ball.

Which he did.

Everything seemed to happen at once after that. Hutch feeling the ball in his glove, somehow getting to his knees, getting off a sidearm throw from his knees, and putting something on it. Cody would say later that the kid had been slow coming out of the box, like he was sure he'd hit a single up the middle. Or maybe he just didn't think there was a second baseman in Legion ball who had enough arm to get him from there.

Hutch did.

His throw to Tommy O'Neill, their first baseman tonight, beat the guy by two steps.

Inning over.

The game stayed 4–0.

Hutch had kept the game from turning into a total blowout.

For now.

"Some of those guys on the Yankees look like they're in *college*," Cody said as they ran off the field, high-fiving Hutch with his glove.

Hutch said, "Tell me about it. I think the guy who hit the home run got lost on his way to the nineteen-and-under game."

"And he's not as big as their starter," Cody said when they got to the bench. "Check it out."

The Yankees starter must have sprinted to the mound as soon as the ump at first made the out call. Hutch recognized him as the No. 5 hitter in their batting order, and could see that he was easily the biggest pitcher they had faced all season.

"Well, you know what they say," Hutch said. "The bigger they are, the harder they fall."

"Tell you what," Cody said. "Find out who 'they' are and see if they want to grab a bat against the Hulkster."

The Hulkster struck out the side in the first. He got Alex Reyes, then Brett, then Hutch on a 2-2 pitch that looked pretty sweet coming out of the guy's hand—he'd heard the infielders calling the Yankees pitcher Ronnie by then—and then just exploded up into Hutch's eyes when it got to the plate.

He looked totally helpless, clueless really, swinging right through it.

When he came back to the bench to get his glove, Cody knew enough not to say anything.

All Hutch said was "Next time," and ran out to second.

Next time was the bottom of the fourth, the Yankees ahead 5–0 by now. By Hutch's count, Ronnie had struck out eight and hadn't given up a hit. But Alex beat out a bunt to start the Cardinals' fourth and Brett worked a walk by laying off the high stuff, watching as the last four pitches Ronnie threw him sailed out of the strike zone like Frisbees.

Hutch's turn.

He knew he wasn't going to bring the Cards all the way back with one at-bat. He just wanted to be ready if the Hulkster threw one in the strike zone, put a good swing on the ball, drive it somewhere and give Darryl a chance to do the same thing behind him.

Hutch did more than put a good swing on a 1-1 fastball.

He put his *best* swing on the sucker.

Caught it right on the sweet spot. Now it wasn't a fastball exploding up and in on him. It was the ball exploding off Hutch's *bat*, making him think in that moment of something guys said shooting hoops:

Butter.

Hutch knew he had caught it, knew he had hit it high and deep toward the alley in left center, knew it might have the legs to get out of the park, knew he had the power to do that at Santaluces, even to the power alleys. He still ran. Hutch never stopped to admire the flight of the ball, never posed at home plate.

He didn't hesitate now the way the kid had in the top of the first.

He busted it out of the box.

Hard.

The next time he allowed himself a look toward the outfield was when he came around first. That's when he saw that both the center fielder and left fielder weren't running anymore, they were just standing near the warning track.

From behind him, Hutch heard Mr. Cullen, coaching first, say something one of the guys on *SportsCenter* used to say.

"It's deep and I don't think it's playable," Mr. Cullen said.

Hutch slowed down, but not too much, not wanting to act like he was trying to show up the other team with some dopey home run trot. He did have a brief urge to pump his fist, just because his team was back in the game now. Didn't do that, either. Just put his head down and kept going, slapped five to Brett's dad, their third-base coach, as he went past him, gave a quick fist-bump to Darryl as he crossed the plate, ran into the crowd of Cardinals waiting for him in front of their bench.

Cody grabbed him from behind and shook him so hard that Hutch's red batting helmet, his lucky one, one that looked older than he was, went flying.

"That sucker flew out of here like a *golf* ball!" Cody said.

Hutch said, "I just closed my eyes and swung."

"Yeah, right," Cody said. "You know what went over the wall along with the ball? The Hulkster's *mojo*."

"Don't be so sure," Hutch said. "There's a lot of ball left to be played, and we're still down two."

Then Darryl doubled to right center, Hank Harding singled him home, and just like that they were only down one, 5–4.

• • •

Tripp was getting stronger as the game went along, the way he did sometimes, even on nights when he didn't give up four runs in the first. But Ronnie of the Yankees had settled back down, too, after Hank's RBI single. The game stayed at 5–4 through the fifth and sixth.

Hutch had walked on four pitches with two outs in the sixth, and then Darryl gave one a ride to dead center, Hutch thinking it had a chance to go out. But as he came around third, he saw the center fielder catch up with the ball in front of the fence in dead center.

Still 5–4.

Stayed that way through the seventh.

Just like that, first game of the regionals, there was a chance that they were six outs away from being through. That's the way it was in knockout tournament baseball. Mr. Cullen had Tripp on a pitch count and had pulled him after he pitched through the top of the seventh. And even though they were still behind by a run, Mr. Cullen decided to go with their closer, Pedro, right there.

In the bottom of the eighth, the Yankees brought in a reliever of their own, the one small guy they seemed to have on their team, a lefty who'd been playing right field. He proceeded to breeze through the bottom of the Cardinals' order by throwing nothing but junk, getting out Cody, Paul Garner and Tripp, who'd moved over to play first base. Sometimes it happened that way, Hutch knew. You waited the whole game to get the hard thrower out of there, then the next kid looked like he was lobbing softballs in there underhanded, and your timing was completely messed up.

Pedro Mota breezed through the middle of the Yankees' order in the top of the ninth, and it stayed a one-run game.

The Cardinals were up against it. Big-time. Except that the first game of the regionals wasn't like their last game in the county tournament. This time they were the ones trying to come from behind. This time it was them who needed one run to get the game into extra innings, two to get to the regional semis.

Or come up empty and go home.

Mr. Cullen gathered the whole team around him before Alex Reyes, their leadoff guy, started off the ninth.

"We're gonna win this thing right here," he said. "Alex is gonna get on and so is Brett, and then we'll see how the little guy likes facing our boppers."

He meant Hutch and Darryl.

Now Mr. Cullen put his hand out, and they all put their hands in there with him, and at the same time everybody yelled, "Cards!"

"Cards on the table is more like it," Cody said to Hutch.

"All in," Hutch said.

The third baseman for the Yankees was right on top of Alex, remembering the bunt he'd laid down earlier. He came in even closer when Alex shortened up again, then had no chance when Alex pulled the bat back and chopped one past him into left field.

Brett Connors next. He was the best they had at making the other pitcher work, taking a lot of pitches. He did that now, working the count full.

Darryl had come out to stand with Hutch in the on-deck circle while Brett was at the plate. Hutch knew that was against the rules. Only one guy was supposed to be standing

43

there. But this was another case of Darryl, looking as relaxed as could be leaning on his bat, acting as if there was a different set of rules for him.

"Must be a slow night for the *Palm Beach Post*," he said to Hutch before the 3-2 pitch to Brett.

Hutch wasn't sure he'd heard him correctly. Most of his energy, *all* of his energy, had been directed toward Brett at the moment, as he tried to will him into taking ball four.

Or hitting one out of sight.

"*What?*" he said to Darryl.

"I was just sayin' that I see the *Post* has got the reporter and the photographer here who covered some of my school games," Darryl said. "Got a crew here from that Channel 12, too. How about that?"

Hutch wanted to say, How about we focus on getting a couple of runs?

What he did say was: "Let's give them a story about us coming from behind in the bottom of the ninth to win the game."

The lefty surprised Brett with a fastball then, one he hadn't shown anybody yet, and Brett swung right through it.

One out, one on, for Hutch.

"You just get on base somehow," Darryl said, calm and cool as ever, smiling that smile of his, like the joke was on the rest of the world. "Then let D-Will take it from there. I'm gonna be all *over* the news tomorrow."

Hutch tapped Darryl's bat with his and said he was cool with that.

He started walking slowly toward the plate.

Then, for some reason, he stopped and turned and saw his dad.

His dad was sitting there at the top row of the aluminum bleachers, leaning back against the railing the way he leaned back against the couch when he was watching a Marlins game. Hutch's mom was sitting to his left, Cody's parents next to her.

Hutch thought: The only thing missing is a can of beer in his hand.

But for some reason, he heard his dad's voice inside his head now, giving him the same advice he always gave when Hutch asked him, doing the only coaching he ever did with Hutch.

Don't try to pull everything. You're better off hitting to right.

When Hutch got into the batter's box, he rubbed some dirt on his bat handle. He didn't wear a batting glove, even though some guys on their team wore two. Just one more old-school thing with him, like wearing his red stirrup socks high.

Hutch dug in.

The lefty tried to get him to chase a dinky pitch, off the outside corner by a foot. Hutch took it for ball one. Then the kid basically threw him the same pitch again, one that was still outside, though not by as much.

The ump called it a strike.

"Hey, ump," Mr. Cullen called down from the first-base coach's box. "That pitch was closer to me than to my kid."

The ump was out from behind the plate in a shot, taking

his mask right off, using it to point at Mr. Cullen. "Zip it, Coach. *Now.*"

Mr. Cullen wasn't quite ready to let it go. He smiled, walked down about ten feet from the coach's box, said, "Just making an observation."

"Keep your observations to yourself the rest of the way."

"Sorry to have mentioned it," Mr. Cullen said, walking back toward first.

Sometimes he'd get into it with an umpire, even for an exchange as brief as that one had been, just to get a pitcher out of his rhythm. Hutch just stayed where he was, deep breathing, the bat resting on his shoulder, trying to think along with the pitcher. He guessed that the kid was going to keep the ball down and away, remembering what had happened when the Hulkster came in on him his second time up.

The lefty tried to go away again.

This one really did catch part of the plate. Or would have if Hutch, going the other way with it the way his dad had told him to, hadn't laid all over it.

Like he was the one who'd gotten the mattress ball.

Hutch hadn't been sure about his first home run of the night, not until he saw that the outfielders had stopped running.

He was sure about this one.

He still ran hard to first, because that was the way you were supposed to play ball.

But this baby was gone.

Gone, baby, gone.

This one was in his sight lines the whole way. This time

he saw the whole thing: The Yankees right fielder stopping dead in his tracks after a few steps. Then the right fielder dropping to one knee as the ball left the yard.

By the time Hutch rounded second base, he didn't feel like he was running at all.

More like he was floating.

Cardinals 6, Yankees 5.

Two dingers in the same game.

He thought of the Spanish word his mom liked to use when something made her particularly happy:

¡Chévere!

Excellent.

Most excellent.

The whole team was waiting for him at home plate, everybody jumping and pounding on each other as Hutch rounded third. Hutch saw the guy with the Channel 12 television camera standing a few feet away, shooting the whole thing, saw the reporter with the microphone in his hand standing next to him.

When Hutch was halfway down the line, he saw the reporter tap the cameraman on the shoulder with his mike, saw the cameraman nod and turn.

Then a TV camera was pointed straight at Hutch for the first time in his life.

Yeah.

Hutch was definitely floating.

HUTCH WAS WATCHING THE HIGHLIGHTS ON CHANNEL 12'S ELEVEN o'clock news along with his mom and dad.

And Cody.

When they showed Hutch's game-winning swing, he stole a look at his dad, thinking this would be a baseball thing that might actually make him smile.

All he did was nod.

They didn't have TiVo in the Hutchinson house, it being too expensive, but they did have an old-fashioned VCR taping the sports report.

Now they were watching the part where Hutch was running straight at the camera after he rounded third.

Connie Hutchinson said, "Could we pick up our head a little, so the world can see that gorgeous face?"

"Mom," Hutch said. "I thought I was just helping us win a ball game, I didn't know I was starring in some *movie."*

On the screen now, Hutch was standing next to the Channel 12 reporter.

"Hush now," his mom said, "they're going to interview you."

"Keith Hutchinson," the reporter said, "what did that feel like, bringing your team back with one swing of the bat?"

The Hutch on TV looked as if he wanted to look anywhere except at the camera before finally mumbling, "It felt good."

In a quiet voice behind him, Hutch heard his mom say, "Like father, like son."

Hutch and Cody were sitting on the floor, in front of the couch. Now Cody fell over on his side, like somebody had shoved him down, grabbed his head with both hands.

"It felt *good*?" he said. "That was the best you could do? You hit a ball like that in the bottom of the ninth and you felt . . . *good*?"

"What was I supposed to say?" Hutch said.

Cody said, "You need to think about using me as a translator from now on, like some of the Japanese players have. Now that you're a celebrity we can't have you thinking for yourself."

When the piece ended, Hutch's mom rewound the tape, Cody telling her to stop when she got back to the celebration at home plate.

"You see me?" he said, getting up and pointing at the corner of the screen. "Right there!"

Hutch's dad got up off the couch. "Where?" he said, squinting. "All the bouncing boys look alike to me."

"I was the one on the right, Mr. Hutchinson," Cody said, looking so sad it was like somebody had canceled his birthday. "You really couldn't tell it was me?"

"Maybe when I watch it again I can go frame by frame."

Then he said he was going to bed, he had to get up early in the morning to go to work.

Hutch watched his mom's eyes follow his dad all the way

out of the room, saw her sad eyes. Sometimes there was a look on her face like she thought he was going to walk out of the room and the house and never come back.

They sat and watched the piece all the way through, at the part now where the sports guy was standing off to the side while the Cardinals kept celebrating in the background, the celebration mostly consisting of the rest of the guys pounding on Hutch.

"I don't see how somebody would say they can't see me," Cody said.

Connie Hutchinson hushed him again, saying she wanted to hear what the reporter said.

"You just heard it, like, two seconds ago," Hutch said.

"And now I want to hear it again," she said.

"There was another Hutch Hutchinson who came out of East Boynton once, and I covered him when I first got to Channel 12," the reporter was saying now. "And a lot of people, myself included, thought he was the best ballplayer to ever come out of this area. But there was a new star tonight, for his old team, Post 226, and it was his son. Reporting from Santaluces Park, this is Steve Carey, Channel 12 Sports."

Now Hutch's mom shut off the TV.

"Okay, time for bed, star," Hutch's mom said. "You, too, Cody."

Cody stood up. "Tell me you saw me when we replayed it, Mrs. H."

She smiled at him, the sad eyes gone, at least for now. "You *definitely* jumped the highest."

"You make me sound like a cheerleader," he said.

"There's nothing wrong with team spirit," she said, still smiling at him. "Now I want both of you team members to head up."

Hutch got up and hugged his mom, and as he did she said, "I'm proud of you."

"What about Dad?" he said.

"He was, too," she said. "But you know your father. He has a hard time expressing himself sometimes."

Hutch thought:

Sometimes?

At least his dad had showed up. He had cared enough tonight to do that.

In a lot of ways, it was like baseball, if you really thought about it.

You took what they gave you.

• • •

Cody was on the air mattress that just barely fit between Hutch's bed and the outside wall of his room. Hutch was on the bed. His mom had let them bring one of the downstairs fans up with them, so Cody could get some cool air on him, too.

They were talking quietly in the darkness, the room lit only by a big moon, both Hutch and Cody trying to keep their voices underneath the sound of the two fans. It was 12:30 in the morning by now, and they didn't want Hutch's parents to hear that they were still awake.

Even having to whisper, the two of them were completely

happy like this, lying on their backs, one of them on a real bed and one of them on the floor, going back over the game a pitch at a time, like it was one of those replays of Marlins games you got on television as soon as the real game was over, until they couldn't keep their eyes open a minute longer.

"Good night, *compai*," Hutch said. His mom had told him that *compai* was the slang version of *compadre*.

"Good night, hero."

Nobody talked then. Hutch fought sleep for one more minute, still picturing that last swing, remembering the way the ball felt coming off his bat, remembering the run around the bases.

Remembering, word for word, what Steve Carey of Channel 12 had said about him and his dad at the end of that sports report.

Especially the part about him being the new Hutch Hutchinson.

It was something his dad never called him.

• • •

It turned out Darryl had been right

Yesterday must have been a *really* slow day for sports news in Palm Beach County. Because there it was the next morning, on the front page of the sports section of the *Post*, a big story about the Cardinals' win over Naples.

Next to it was a big color picture of Hutch jumping into that crowd of teammates at home plate, like he was suspended in midair.

The big headline over the story and the picture read this way: "First Round Heroics from Second-Generation Star."

The sports section was waiting for Hutch and Cody on the kitchen table, along with what Cody immediately described, in Cody-speak, as a "ginormous" stack of pancakes.

Carl Hutchinson had already gone off to Emerald Dunes to caddy.

Cody pointed to the picture of Hutch.

"At least they shot you from your best side," he said.

"All's you can basically see is the number two on the back of my uniform," Hutch said.

Jeter's number.

"Like I said," Cody said, going right for the pancakes. "Your best side."

They put their chairs together so they could both read the story, which started out with the writer talking about how the son of former American Legion star Carl Hutchinson had turned Santaluces Park into his own field of dreams last night.

"Field of dreams," Cody said. "It's practically like I wrote it myself."

"Except for the fact that it's punctuated properly," Hutch said.

Cody just turned and stared at him.

"C'mon," Hutch said. "That was funny."

"No, *this* is funny," Cody said, and opened a mouth full of half-chewed pancakes so Hutch could see.

"I'm only looking at the paper," Hutch said, "so I never have to look at you ever again."

The writer must have done his homework because there was a lot in there about his dad. Near the end of the story, the writer even mentioned that Carl Hutchinson had recently assumed a "new position" with the Sun Coast Driving Service.

Like he was Hutch, assuming a new position at second base.

Nothing in there about him being a caddy at Emerald Dunes.

Connie Hutchinson said, "That's the biggest write-up in the papers you've ever gotten, hon."

"Mom," Hutch said, "this whole thing is getting mad embarrassing now. The guy makes it out like I was some sort of one-man team last night."

Mouth still full, Cody said something that ended with " . . . hit two bombs."

"Seriously, Mom," Hutch said, because this was bothering him. "I don't want the other guys to think that because I had one good game and answered a few questions that I'm looking for attention."

"Sometimes you don't have anything to say about it," she said, then put a hand on his shoulder and gave it a squeeze. "Sometimes attention comes looking for you."

He looked up at her. "Did Dad see the story before he left?"

"I don't know," she said. "The paper was open when I came downstairs, but he was already gone."

"You think he was cool with the way they talked about him?"

His mom said, "I'm sure your father is as proud of you as I am."

"Know what I'm sure of?" Cody said.

"What?"

"How excited the rest of us are going to be just to be on the same field today with . . . *the* . . . *new* . . . *American* . . . *Idol!*"

Hutch put his head down so his forehead was resting on the sports section of the *Post*.

"Make him stop, Mom," he said.

"Too big a job for me, *mi cucubano*," she said.

One of her many nicknames for Hutch, this one meaning "firefly."

Hutch said to Cody, "I didn't ask for any of this, you know."

He felt Cody patting him on the back.

"No," he said, "you certainly didn't."

Then Cody laughed and said, "But you're still gonna get it."

"Look," Paul Garner said, pointing from behind the pitcher's mound, as Hutch and Cody came walking out of the parking lot at Caloosa Park toward the field named after Lou Gehrig. "Isn't that the kid I saw on *SportsCenter* last night?"

"Don't start," Hutch yelled back.

Garner, grinning, said, "You must be joking. I'm just *getting* started."

Hank Harding, who usually didn't say much more than "nice hit" or "nice play," joined right in.

"I recognize the second-generation star," he said, putting air quotes with his fingers around *second-generation star.* "But who's the guy with him?"

Brett said, "The ugly guy? Never saw him before."

Cody made a bring-it-on motion with his hands. "Go ahead, make your silly comments, you little, little boys," he said. "Me and the star can take it."

Hutch turned. "You, too?"

Cody shrugged. "Slipped out."

"Do you plan to practice with us today, Hutch?" Alex Reyes said. "Or are you too tired from carrying us to victory?"

"Can we get you something?" Brett said. "Something to drink, maybe?"

"A new bike?" Hank said.

"If you want to rest on your . . . laurels and take it easy," Paul said, "that's fine with us."

"Wait, I've got an idea," Cody said. "Why don't all you comedians *kiss* his . . . laurels."

Hutch laughed along with everybody else. Eventually his teammates let up on him and they all started to warm up, the conversation shifting to their next game, against Sarasota, to be played down in Fort Lauderdale.

Darryl was the last one to show up, right before Mr. Cullen did.

As usual, it was as if he just appeared, out of nowhere, or got beamed in the way guys did in one of the old *Star Trek* shows that Hutch liked to watch on the Sci Fi Channel. They'd just look up and there would be Darryl, bat bag slung over his shoulder, wearing his Nike flip-flops. Even if it was one of their late practices, way after the sun had gone down, he'd still be wearing some pair of cool sunglasses, never the same pair two days in a row. Hutch didn't know a lot about fashion, or what things cost, but Cody did, and he had told Hutch one day that the pair of Oakley glasses Darryl was wearing cost more than both their baseball gloves combined.

Today Darryl was wearing the kind of glasses you sometimes saw big leaguers wearing, the kind that seemed to just fit your face like a mask even though they weren't really attached anyplace.

"A-Rod glasses," Cody said.

"Very cool."

"Just not as cool as Darryl."

They watched from the field as Darryl sat down on the bench, let them all see him taking a brand-new pair of black Nike baseball shoes out of the box, holding them up and admiring them before he started lacing them up, taking his time doing that, as if the laces had to be perfect. You've got to hand it to the guy, Hutch thought. He *is* cool. A couple of minutes before practice and he still acted as if he had all day to gear up.

Brett was hitting fly balls to the outfielders and Hutch was out there shagging with them, just for the fun of it.

"On time for Darryl," Cody said, "is pretty much when he gets here."

"He's not late," Hutch said. "So just chill."

Cody was already dripping wet with sweat, as he usually was about five minutes after he started doing any kind of running.

"Chill," he said. "In this heat. Out*standing* advice."

Cody ran back a few steps then backhanded a ball, threw it all the way in to Brett on one bounce—for a guy who'd mostly played second base in his life, he had a surprisingly good arm—and then said to Hutch, "I just hope Darryl sticks up for you the way you do for him, especially when you're not around."

"We're on the same team," Hutch said. "Why wouldn't he?"

"'Cause even though we're on the same team, dude, he

acts as if he's in a whole different league than the rest of us, that's why."

It was time for what Mr. Cullen called their "situation room" drills.

"Situation room" drills were game situations. Coach would leave the regular defense out there and use a couple of the pitchers and guys off the bench to run the bases. Sometimes it would be one guy on base, sometimes two, sometimes bases loaded. Then Mr. Cullen would call out how many outs there were, what inning it was, and what the score was, before hitting the ball somewhere.

If it were a single to the outfield with, say, two runners on, the guy picking up the ball would have to make a decision about trying to throw a runner out at either third or home. If he had no play, he'd be expected to throw to the right base, or hit the cutoff man.

Or else.

Or else they'd do the exact same play again and keep doing it until they got it right. The base runners had to make the right decisions, too, read where the ball was and who was throwing it before they'd try to take an extra base or try to run all the way home.

Sometimes Mr. Cullen would keep the play in the infield. Put a runner on first, another on third, saying a double play ended a one-run game. On plays like that, he'd put a runner behind Brett, let him take off for first as soon as the ball was hit.

Right now, it was first and third, nobody out. Mr. Cullen

rocketed one up the gap in right center between Alex Reyes and Cody, neither one of them having a chance to catch the ball on the fly. It landed between them and looked like it was going to make it all the way to the wall before Cody cut it off with a sliding stop. Then he scrambled to his feet and made a perfect cutoff throw to Hutch, who'd nearly sprinted all the way out to Cody's normal position in right to meet the ball.

"Home!" Hutch heard from behind him, not just one voice, but a lot of them.

As soon as Hutch had the ball in his glove he was transferring it to his throwing hand as quickly as he did when trying to turn a fast double play, was wheeling and throwing the ball toward Brett without even looking, as if his teammates were right about him when they said he had eyes in the back of his head.

From where he was in short right, he shouldn't have been able to get it to Brett on the fly without setting himself.

But he did.

Paul Garner, who had pretty good speed, was the runner trying to score all the way from first, but when he saw how badly the throw had beaten him, he didn't even slide. No point.

When Hutch jogged back to second, Darryl came over and got down on his knees, and started making the I-am-notworthy motion you saw fans making in the stands at sporting events sometimes.

"Oh, *Captain*," he said. "No wonder the papers and the TV love you so much."

"Cut it out," Hutch said, grinning.

Darryl stayed where he was. He never showed you anything on the field. But he was making a big show now. And if his plan was to embarrass Hutch, it was a solid one.

"Is that a direct order, *Captain Hutch*?"

"Seriously, dude," Hutch said. "Get up."

"Just trying to treat you the same way the me-di-a does, *Captain*."

Finally he got to his feet, smiling at Hutch as he did, as if it were all a big joke. And Hutch figured it was, except for the way he had kept leaning on *Captain* the way he did. Nobody on the team ever referred to Hutch that way, especially not Darryl Williams.

Until now.

They waited near second base while Mr. Cullen brought in Cody to do some running and sent Paul out to replace him in right, even though left was normally Paul's position.

Hutch said, "I'm sure the *Post* and Channel 12 have lost interest in me already."

Still, Darryl wouldn't let up.

"Big star like you?" he said, still with that smile on his face. "They'll lose interest in Britney Spears or Beyoncé 'fore they lose interest in you."

Before Darryl could say anything else, Mr. Cullen was calling out the next situation, and they were back to baseball.

This should have been boring stuff, going through one situation after another like this. Only nothing about baseball ever bored Hutch, not even the waiting time. It was why he never dogged it even when some of the other guys did, never just went through the motions, never took shortcuts even if the play was somewhere else, or if he thought Mr. Cullen might not be watching. He prided himself on being where he was supposed to be at all times, the way Jeter of the Yankees always was.

Hutch always remembered the famous flip play Jeter had made in the playoffs one time, against the Oakland A's.

The Yankees were down 0–2 in the first round, needing a win to keep the series going, when one of the A's hit a ball to the outfield. Jeremy Giambi, Jason Giambi's brother, tried to score on the play. Looked like he *would* score. Only here came Jeter, the shortstop, flashing toward the first-base line, picking up the ball that had gone over the cutoff man's head, making that neat backhand flip to the Yankees catcher, Jorge Posada, who put the tag on Giambi.

The Yankees came back to win the series, and lots of people thought Jeter's play turned the whole series around.

Hard to say for certain.

What *was* certain was this:

Jeter was where he was *supposed* to be, backing up the cutoff man. He was able to make one of the most famous plays in Yankee's history, *baseball* history, because he did something in the moment that he had probably done hundreds of times in a drill that a lot of his Yankee teammates probably thought was more boring than ballet.

So Hutch kept going to the right place today, even though most of the action seemed to be running through Darryl. When Darryl made a pretty amazing relay throw of his own to the plate, from his knees, getting Cody at the plate when he should have had no shot, Hutch said, "You the man, D."

Darryl responded in a voice loud enough to be heard at the Little League field next door. "Oh no, *Captain*. How can I be the man when *you* the man?"

Hutch decided then he was basically going to shut up for the rest of practice. Darryl seemed locked on this Captain routine no matter what Hutch said.

Mr. Cullen gave them a break a few minutes after that, told them to go get a drink, because when they were done with their little break, they were going right into what he called Extreme Infield.

Just about everybody on the field except Hutch groaned at that particular news bulletin.

Extreme Infield, the Cardinals knew, was as much a drill for hard baserunning as it was for fielding the ball and making the proper plays. If the runners had the chance to slide hard and break up a double play—cleanly—they were supposed to do it. If they had a chance to go hard into Brett at the plate, they were supposed to do that. Tripp said Extreme Infield was like a drill his basketball coach would use sometimes, putting a bunch of guys under the basket and telling them to do whatever they had to do to get a rebound, short of assault and battery.

The Cardinals did Extreme Infield for about fifteen minutes, with only a few knockdowns at home plate and no need for the first-aid kit, which Hutch always saw as a huge positive. Finally Mr. Cullen announced that they could quit for the day if Darryl and Hutch could turn one last double play.

"Bottom of the ninth," he said. "We're up a run. First and third. Double play sends us off the field a winner. But, and this is a big but . . . "

Cody, who'd been sent out to second to run, raised his hand. "As big as Tripp's?"

The rest of the guys laughed. So did Mr. Cullen, even though you could see he didn't want to.

"Where was I?" he said.

"Tripp's big old—" Cody said.

"*But*," Mr. Cullen continued, "you gotta be sure you can turn two. I'm gonna play you a couple of feet back off the grass. Not quite double-play depth but close enough, like we do sometimes. If the ball's not hit hard enough, come home and cut off the tying run."

Then he proceeded to hit a hard grounder to Darryl's left.

As soon as Hutch saw where the ball was, he was as sure as Mr. C wanted him to be that they could get the double play.

Easy.

In addition to everything else Darryl Williams had going for him, size and speed and strength, he also had the softest hands for an infielder Hutch had ever seen on a kid their age. Even softer than Hutch's. Now he fielded the ball with his glove hand. As he did, Hutch slowed down just slightly, wanting to have the timing just right, wanting to set his feet on each side of the bag just as Darryl turned and gave him one of his perfect underhand flips, wanting to be balanced as Hutch himself turned to avoid the runner and make the relay throw to first.

Tommy O'Neill, who could play just about any position for them, was the one pretending to be the batter running toward first, and he was one of their slowest guys. Brett Connors, Hutch knew, was coming from first like a city bus.

Hutch got to second with plenty of time to spare.

The ball didn't.

It was still in Darryl's glove.

Hutch knew he had to hang in there, even knowing Brett would take him out with a clean slide if he could, because that was the way Brett played the game.

Come *on*, D, Hutch thought.

Gimme the rock.

The only thing Hutch could figure was that even with those soft, sure hands, Darryl couldn't get the ball out of his glove. Now the double play was out of the question.

Hutch just wanted to get one, get the ball in time to keep Alex Reyes, halfway down the line at third, from scoring the fake tying run.

Maybe it didn't matter to the other guys, but it mattered to Hutch.

Finally Darryl had the ball in his bare hand. Hutch saw that, thought he even saw Darryl smiling right before he let it go, like maybe he was embarrassed to have messed up on what was such a routine play, at least for him.

Except he was still messing it up.

He didn't flip the ball underhand the way he usually did when he was moving toward second. Instead he lollipopped the ball *over*hand, the ball floating toward Hutch like a balloon.

This was one time when Hutch didn't need those eyes in the back of his head. He was sure he was going to get popped.

He was right.

This time he didn't have to pretend he was flying, the way he had the night before, after he'd hit that game-winning home run.

This time Hutch really was.

When he came down, he came down on his right shoulder.

It was a hard enough landing that he felt his breath come out of him as soon as he hit the infield dirt. As baked out as that dirt was in the summer, no matter how much they watered it at Caloosa, it was the same as if he'd landed in the parking lot.

Brett was kneeling next to him almost right away, saying how sorry he was, asking if Hutch was okay, wanting to know where it hurt, trying to get all those things out at once.

Looking as if he was in more pain than Hutch was at the moment.

"I kept expecting you to turn and get out of the way as you made the relay, like you always do," Brett said. "But you never turned around."

Hutch wanted to tell him that it's pretty tough making a relay throw if you don't have the ball, but he needed to get a *lot* more air in his lungs before he could do that.

He tried to sit up instead, hoping that would help him catch his breath faster.

Mr. Cullen was there by now.

"Easy, tiger," he said, kneeling next to Brett.

Cody was standing behind them, staring down at Hutch, eyes wide.

"Let's take this nice and slow," Mr. Cullen said, putting his arm behind Hutch's shoulders and gently lifting him up. "You hit your head?"

Hutch coughed, took in some air, coughed again. "No," he managed.

"You sure? This infield is like cement."

Hutch said, "I hit my shoulder. It's like my dad says. Didn't get my flaps down."

"Somebody get an ice pack out of the kit," Mr. Cullen said, and Cody went running toward the bench like he was trying to go from first to third.

Brett said, "Hutch, I am so sorry, but you know we're supposed to go pedal-to-the-metal in Extreme Infield—"

Hutch put a hand up to stop him, wincing a little, unable to help it, as he raised his arm.

"You did what I would have done if I were coming into second," he said. "No worries." And bumped him some fist.

"You *always* get out of the way, every single time," Brett said.

"Well," Hutch said, "there's a first time for everything."

Cody came back with the ice. Hutch put the pack right on top of his shoulder, where it hurt the most, thinking Mr. Cullen was right: As hard as the infield was, he was lucky he hadn't broken something.

He stood up now, feeling somebody pulling him by his left arm.

Darryl.

"Sorry, Captain," he said. "Couldn't get the dang ball out of my glove."

"I noticed," Hutch said.

Darryl said, "Didn't mean to cause no accidents."

"No worries," Hutch said again.

"That," Mr. Cullen said, "is about as extreme as Extreme Infield should get." Then he told Hutch to go take a seat on the bench and keep that ice on his shoulder, and anybody who wanted to take some extra batting practice could. He'd give each guy three swings until pickup time.

Cody walked with Hutch to the bench. When he was sure nobody could hear them, he said, "How bad is it, really?"

"I'm fine," Hutch said.

"You sure?" Cody said. "Because the way you landed, not breaking your fall—"

"I said I'm fine!" Hutch said, the words coming out with more teeth on them, sharper, than he intended.

"Okay then," Cody said.

"Okay," Hutch said.

They walked the rest of the way to the bench in silence.

• • •

Hutch didn't say much on the ride home, the ice pack still on his shoulder.

When they got to the Hesters', they ate burgers that Mr. Hester had cooked on the tiny grill in their tiny backyard.

After dinner Hutch and Cody went to Cody's bedroom in the back of the house and watched a couple of old episodes of *24* on Cody's computer.

When it was time for Hutch to go home, Cody walked him outside.

It felt like the temperature had dropped about ten degrees since dinner, which in Florida, especially in the summer, probably meant another thunderstorm was about to blow through. And right then, as if on cue, they saw a flash of lightning in the distance, heard the distant rumble of thunder.

It was then that Hutch put a voice to the question that had been running through his mind. Or at least part of the question.

"Why do you think Darryl was messing with me today?"

"You mean calling you 'Captain' over and over again?"

"Yeah," Hutch said.

"I told you last night I *thought* he was torked off, *compai*," Cody said. "I think this was just his way of *saying* it."

Hutch hadn't felt much like smiling since Brett had sent him flying. But anytime he heard Cody using Spanish expressions, even one word, Hutch couldn't help himself.

"So what do I do about it?"

"Nothing," Cody said. "Darryl's Darryl. And he ain't changin', dude."

"What's his *problem*?" Hutch said.

There was more lightning, getting closer. Hutch knew he'd better get a move on if he didn't want to get real wet, real quick.

Now Hutch saw Cody's smile in the light from the sky.

"You really want to know?" Cody said.

"Yeah, I do."

"You're too good."

"But he's better," Hutch said.

"Maybe not by enough."

Hutch almost said something else, something he'd been wanting to say since practice, but he didn't. Instead he bumped fists with Cody and headed home.

He got there about a minute before the storm hit. His dad was in the living room, and before Hutch saw what was on the television he knew, because he could see the can of beer on the small table at the end of the couch.

Hutch gave a little knock on the wall, like he was asking permission to enter, saw that it was the Marlins-Cubs game his dad was watching.

Saw that the force field was up.

"Hey," his dad said, shooting him a quick look, taking a sip of his beer.

"Hey."

"I'm only watching an inning or two before *Law and Order*."

"Cool."

His dad wasn't Spanish, liked to say that his nationality was Florida redneck. But all the time he had spent in the sun his whole life had made him almost as dark as Hutch, almost as dark as Consuela Valentin Hutchinson.

"What's the score?" Hutch said.

"Five–four in the third."

Hutch lingered in the doorway, wanting this night to be different from all the others, wanting to be invited in.

Wanting to talk about baseball with his dad tonight as much as he ever had.

His dad turned back around, as if realizing that Hutch was still standing there.

"Something on your mind?"

Go ahead, you loser.

Tell him.

"Nah," Hutch said.

"'Night then," his dad said.

"'Night."

Hutch went to his bedroom, closed the door, reached under his bed and found the brochure for The Hun School of Princeton, up in New Jersey, the brochure he'd sent away for without telling anybody, not even his mom. The Hun School of Princeton: With white buildings that looked like they belonged in the nicest parts of Palm Beach, and happy-looking students, and streams, and trees, like something out of another world.

The famous boarding school that was supposed to have one of the best baseball programs in the whole country, as good as anything in Florida or California, even though it was in the Northeast.

Hutch heard people talk all the time about how cold it could get up north in the winter, even watched the Weather Channel sometimes so he could see the pictures when one of those big storms they called Nor'easters hit.

Maybe so.

Hutch didn't care.

It couldn't be colder than what he'd felt tonight at practice, what he was still feeling now, even on a hot Florida night. Hutch hadn't said this to Cody. He'd thought about saying it to his dad just now in the living room, before he lost his nerve.

But how could anything be colder than what Darryl Williams had done tonight?

Holding that ball on purpose.

Hutch knew he couldn't prove it.

He just *knew*.

Darryl had wanted him to get run over.

WHEN HUTCH CAME DOWN FOR BREAKFAST, IT WAS JUST HIS MOM in the kitchen, almost ready to leave for the clothing store she worked at, called Blue, at the Crystal Tree Plaza in North Palm.

"How's my boy today?" she said.

Connie Hutchinson was in a good mood this morning. It seemed no matter what went on with their family, his mom had the best attitude of anybody Hutch knew.

It was why Hutch tried to never let on when he was in a bad mood. Or having a bad day. Because she *never* seemed to have one, never let the sadness win.

"I'm good," he said. "My shoulder feels a lot better than I thought it was going to this morning."

He had poked his head inside her room before going to bed, and told her what had happened. She had said that if his shoulder hurt any worse when he woke up, she wanted to have the doctor take a look at it.

"Really it does," Hutch added, pouring himself some cereal.

She looked at him. "I didn't say anything."

"I'm just sayin'."

Then he put his head down like he was watching a ball into his glove and made himself *extremely* busy eating Frosted Mini-Wheats.

"Of course with you," his mom said, "it's usually what you're *not* saying."

"You sound like Cody," he said. "Or maybe it's him that sounds like you. I can't decide sometimes."

"Don't talk with your mouth full."

"Okay, that doesn't sound anything like Cody."

She sat down at the table, even though Hutch could see by the clock that she should be heading out the door. Never good. She was staring at him, the way she did sometimes, as if trying to read his mind.

Which she sometimes could, at the weirdest possible times.

"You okay?" she said, smiling at him.

"I told you my shoulder's fine."

"Wasn't talking about your shoulder."

Even with her psychic powers, Hutch told himself there was no way she could know what was really bothering him.

But her radar had picked something up, Hutch could tell. Now she wanted Hutch to open up. She was a mom, after all, which meant she thought you were breaking some sort of law if you *didn't* open up.

"Anything else you want to talk about this morning?" she said. "Anything at all with your old mom?"

"You're not old," Hutch said.

"Don't change the subject."

"I didn't know there was a subject, Mom."

"You have that look."

"The one where I just got up and I'm eating my breakfast?" Hutch said. "*That* look?"

She's the opposite of Dad, he thought. He never wants to talk and she always does.

"The look where something's bothering you."

"Nope."

"If there is . . . "

"You'll be the first to know."

"Right," she said, smiling again.

She stood up, kissed him on the forehead, said she'd pick him and Cody up after practice. She had her hand on the doorknob when Hutch said, "Mom?"

Thinking as he said it that he couldn't help himself sometimes—it was like she wore him down just by knowing him as well as she did.

"You ever wonder why Dad and I hardly ever talk about baseball?"

"I don't wonder," she said. "Maybe because I think I understand."

"Understand what?" Hutch said.

"Understand that he worries that it will break your heart someday the way it broke his."

Hutch said, "But I love baseball."

His mom said, "So did he."

Past tense.

● ● ●

The thing about being a second baseman now—temporarily, Hutch kept telling himself—was that you hardly ever had to make a big throw, the kind shortstops seemed to make all the time.

Maybe once a game, if you were lucky, you had to backhand a ball behind second and gun a throw to first from there.

Or make the kind of relay throw from the outfield he'd made at practice yesterday.

Most of the time, on routine grounders, you felt like you could make your throw to first base underhanded and still get the guy. Or run the ball over there yourself. So even after landing on his shoulder the way he did, Hutch knew he wasn't going to miss the next game. There was about as much of a chance of him missing a game, especially a *tournament* game, as there was of Cal Ripken Jr. missing a game when he had his streak going.

He just didn't want to have to worry about his shoulder every time he made a throw or swung the bat. The only thing he wanted to worry about was beating their next opponent, the Sarasota Dodgers, down in Fort Lauderdale.

No worries, as it turned out. The shoulder was a little stiff for the next couple of days, but not sore. He could throw and he could hit. By the time Hutch and the rest of the guys got on the bus for the trip down 95 to Fort Lauderdale, Hutch pronounced himself good to go.

"Thank you for that bulletin," Cody said, "because the rest of the guys and me were very concerned that you might not be ready to play tonight."

The bus ride took about an hour. They got off at Commercial Boulevard and as they did, Hutch pointed out a huge billboard for the Joe DiMaggio Children's Hospital.

"He used to have a charity softball game every year at Fort Lauderdale Stadium, which is right next to where we're playing tonight," Hutch said.

"I know you think I should know this, but I'm going to ask you anyway, and don't hurt me," Cody said. "Who's Joe DiMaggio?"

Hutch reached over and cuffed him lightly on the back of his head, something he had to do a lot. "He's one of the greatest baseball players of *all time*, a center fielder, known as the Yankee Clipper," Hutch said. "And that didn't hurt."

"'Yankee Clipper' makes him sound like the team barber," Cody said.

Hutch ignored him, saying, "When he was still alive, they used to introduce him as the greatest living ballplayer, even though my dad says it was Willie Mays."

Now Cody brightened. "That must be the guy they named Willie Mays Hayes after in *Major League*."

Hutch closed his eyes, shook his head. "Anyway," he said, "here's the coolest stat of all on Joe DiMaggio: He played in ten World Series and the Yankees won nine of them."

"If one of us has to be up on stuff like that," Cody said, "I'm glad it's you."

Hutch said, "He also had almost the same number of career home runs as he did strikeouts."

"Awesome," Cody said, but in a way that let Hutch know that Cody's brain had already moved off Joe DiMaggio and on to something else. "Hey," he said, frowning, "how come we're not on the big field here?"

"Because you gotta make the finals to make the big field," Hutch said. "Which is the way it oughta be."

They got off at 12ᵗʰ Avenue and passed Fort Lauderdale Stadium. Hank Harding, sitting behind them, said that he had come to an Orioles-Marlins game here in March, and caught a foul ball.

"Just make sure you catch all balls tonight," Cody said.

"You ever think about using your mouth to catch them?" Hank said. "'Cause I'm pretty sure it's bigger than your glove."

The trash-talking among the Cardinals really began after that, and suddenly the inside of their old bus was as loud as recess and everybody was joining in.

Everybody except Darryl, D-Will himself.

He was in the last row, head resting against the window, sunglasses on.

Fast asleep.

This time it was the Cardinals jumping off to the quick lead, 3–0 in the top of the first.

Alex walked, Brett singled to left, and Hutch tripled them both home. At least the man working the public address system called it a triple. Hutch thought it was a double and an error because of the way the center fielder misplayed the ball after it bounced off the wall in left center.

Standing on third, Hutch thought they might be looking at a really big inning, but then Darryl just missed a home run the way he'd just missed one against Naples, the ball falling a few feet from the fence in left.

Problem was, Darryl was sure it was a home run when it left his bat. Which is why he went into his home-run pose at home plate, tossing his bat away, stopping a few feet out of the batter's box, hands on hips, watching the flight of the ball.

The way guys did on *SportsCenter*, every single night.

He was still standing a few feet away from the plate, hadn't even started running yet, when the ball ended up in the left fielder's glove and all he had to show for his swing was a long, *really* long, sacrifice fly.

Hutch thought the ball was going out, too, but tagged up anyway, ran hard for the plate even though the kid had no shot of ever throwing him out.

He ran so hard right through home plate that he nearly ran into Darryl, who had backed up a few feet but was still staring toward the outfield, as if what happened there was some kind of optical illusion.

"Almost," Hutch said, putting the brakes on.

"There's no almost in baseball," Darryl said. "This isn't a game of dang horseshoes. So don't give me any of your *almost*."

"Hey," Hutch said, picking up Darryl's bat for him. "At least we got another run out of it."

Darryl grabbed the bat away from him and said, "Go captain somebody else," and walked away from him.

• • •

In the third inning, the Cardinals were still ahead by a score of 4–2. And they were threatening again, bases loaded, two outs, a chance to blow the roof right off the semis.

Darryl at the plate.

All Hutch had to do was take one look at him from first to see how much he wanted to hit a grand slam.

He laid off the first pitch, thinking it was high, turned and gave the ump a quick look when he called it strike one.

Then he swung through a hard fastball to get into an 0-2 hole. Some pitchers would waste one here, seeing if they could get the hitter to strike himself out.

Not this pitcher. He was big, and had an arm to match.

He went into his windup and came with the exact opposite of a waste pitch, threw one as hard as he could, one of those fastballs that dared you to catch up with it.

Darryl didn't.

He was the one who got wasted, swinging so hard trying to hit his grand slam that he spun himself around and stumbled and nearly ended up in the lap of the Sarasota catcher, his bat falling out of his hands.

From where he stood, a few feet off first, Hutch thought he heard somebody in the infield, either the shortstop or the third baseman, laugh right before the Sarasota guys ran off the field.

Hutch couldn't see who'd done it because he was still watching Darryl.

Who must have heard the laugh, too, because as soon as he had his feet under him again, he glared over toward the Sarasota bench.

"Somebody think this is *funny*?" he said.

Nobody said anything back.

Then suddenly Darryl was picking up his bat in his right hand, pulling it back like he was going to fling it. Not at the Sarasota bench. Just somewhere.

Like he was about to throw it as hard as he'd just swung it.

"Darryl!" Hutch yelled.

Hutch knew he had to stop him somehow, knew that as soon as the bat left Darryl's hand, he was going to be ejected from the game. American Legion rules were clear about that.

And about this: If you got ejected from a game, you were automatically suspended from the next game.

Hutch was running across the infield, between the pitcher's mound and first base, yelling, "Don't!"

But it wasn't Hutch who stopped him.

It was the home plate umpire.

Darryl didn't even know the ump was behind him. But as he tried to launch the bat he couldn't, because the ump had a death grip on the barrel.

Hutch stopped a few feet away, heard the ump in a calm voice say, "No."

Just that.

No.

It stopped Darryl. Or maybe confused him.

Because hardly anyone ever said that word to him.

"We both know you don't really want to do that," the ump said.

The ump was a young black guy, a former ballplayer himself, named Anthony, who had already worked a bunch of their games up around Palm Beach. For a second the two of them just stood there, Anthony and Darryl, each of them holding on to his end of the bat, like they were in a tug-of-war, or had come up with a new way to choose up sides.

Anthony used his free hand to take off his mask, show everybody he was smiling, that he had everything under control.

"I'd like you to let go of the bat, son," Anthony said. "You hearin' me on this?"

When Darryl didn't say anything, Anthony, just loud enough for Darryl—and Hutch—to hear, said, "Answer me when I talk to you, son. Are you hearin' me on this?"

"Yes."

"Yes *sir*, think you meant to say."

"Yes sir," Darryl Williams said, though you could see that he wasn't used to being told what to do any more than he was used to somebody saying no to him.

Darryl let go of the bat. As soon as he did, Anthony handed it right back to him.

"Now go put that thing back in the rack, 'cause we got ourselves a heck of a good ball game goin' here," Anthony said.

Darryl did exactly what the ump told him to do.

Hutch thought it was as amazing as him striking out the way he just had.

Maybe even more.

• • •

Paul Garner, who had started for the Cardinals, left after the fifth with the game tied 5–5. Chris Mahoney, who started in left when Paul pitched, came on after that and shut out the Dodgers through the bottom of the eighth, without allowing a base runner, the best Mahoney had pitched all season by far.

By then the Cardinals were back ahead 7–5 because Brett Connors, who hardly ever hit home runs, had hit an opposite-field dart down the right-field line that was fair by about three feet and cleared the fence by less than that.

It stayed 7–5 into the bottom of the ninth.

Hutch never tried to think past the next pitch when he was in the field. Sometimes he'd pretend he was the manager when the Cardinals were batting, trying to think a few batters ahead. But never when he was in the field. When he was in the field, he was in the moment, thinking what he was doing with the ball if it was hit to him or where he was going if it was hit to somebody else.

Still:

With two outs and nobody on and Pedro Mota having just absolutely gassed the first two Dodger hitters in their half of the ninth, he was actually thinking that they might get to the bus for once with a win that wasn't scarier than a *Saw* movie.

No such luck.

Hank Harding promptly booted a routine ground ball that would have ended the game.

The next Dodger batter hit one in the hole between Hank and Darryl, and Darryl made a sweet play to keep the ball from going into left field. But instead of putting the ball in his pocket, he tried to make a hero throw and get the guy at first.

It exploded out of his hand the way balls usually exploded off his bat, and went over Tripp's head at first and halfway up into the stands. Not only were the Cardinals *not* on their way to the bus, they were looking at second and third and the Dodgers being a hit away from tying the sucker up.

Pedro hadn't done anything wrong except get two ground balls, but you could see he was hot, so Mr. Cullen made a little talking motion with his hand, meaning he wanted Hutch to be the one to settle him down.

When he got to the mound he said, "*Qué pasa,* dude?"

"*Qué* this *stinks!*" Pedro said.

"So how about this," Hutch said, trying to act as relaxed as if they were already having their postgame snack. "How 'bout you get this guy to hit it to me this time, and we get out of Dodge."

Hutch hit him encouragingly with his glove and went back to his position.

Pedro went to 2-2 on the next hitter, the little guy leading off for the Dodgers, then threw him a righteous fastball in on the guy's hands, a pitch that would have been unhittable against a free swinger. Only this guy, the Dodgers' second baseman, was the opposite of that. Hutch had noticed all game long how good he was at handling a bat.

Better now.

Somehow muscling a flare toward short center.

Hutch wasn't off with the crack of the bat, because it wasn't a crack—it was more like a *thud*. He was still on it, focused hard on it, almost seeing inside his head where he thought it was going to land. If it landed. Hutch ran toward that spot, not taking his eyes off the ball for one second, blocking out everything else, going at full speed now, tracking this baby real good.

Knowing he was going to get there.

Getting ready to backhand the ball.

Reaching up with his glove just as Darryl, at full speed reaching for the ball himself, came crashing into him from the other direction.

Two shortstops. Each thinking the exact same thing:

I got it.

By some miracle, they didn't bang heads, make it one of those "helmet to helmet" hits football announcers were always talking about, only without the helmets.

Darryl had angled himself a little bit to Hutch's right, so it was more like shoulder to shoulder.

Hutch still felt like he'd run into a wall.

He ended up flat on his back, Darryl next to him, already groaning his way into a sitting position. The first person Hutch saw when he opened his eyes was the field ump.

"You okay, kid?" the ump said.

"Think so."

"How about you?" he said to Darryl.

"Yeah," Darryl said. "Now that I find out my head's still attached to my body."

The ump looked back at Hutch now. "Then would you mind if I took a look at your glove?"

"My glove . . . ?"

The ump reached down then, opened up the Jeter mitt, the Rawlings PROSDJ2-50 he'd saved up for the whole school year, the 11-1/2" model, the cool-looking black one.

The ball was still in the pocket.

"Well then," the ump said, "this baby is over."

He straightened up, jerked his right fist in the air, yelled, *"Out!"*

Then, just as loud, he yelled, *"Ball game over!"*

For Darryl, it was like an alarm had suddenly gone off. He jumped to his feet, stood over Hutch and pointed a finger at him. "You trying to kill me?"

Hutch was still feeling a little shaky. But he made himself get up, too. As soon as he did, Darryl was right in his face, like a manager in the big leagues getting ready to go at it with the home plate ump.

"I was trying to make a play," Hutch said in a quiet voice.

"Yeah," Darryl said. "On *me*."

Hutch said, "D-Will, I didn't run into you. We ran into each other." Still not yelling, trying to talk to him in a normal voice. Mr. Cullen was there, so were some of the other fielders. They were all giving Hutch and Darryl plenty of room.

"That was *my* ball," Darryl said. "It's *always* the shortstop's ball."

This was the last thing Hutch wanted to be doing, especially after winning a ball game. Not just winning it, but doing it on a crazy play like this. But he wasn't going to let Darryl call him out this way.

"Look at where we're standing," he said. "It was closer to me than it was to you."

It was true, they were a couple of yards to the second base side of the bag.

"I was calling for it," Darryl said. "You're telling me you didn't hear me?"

"I didn't," Hutch said. "Because you didn't."

"You're calling me a liar now?" Darryl said.

"I'm saying if you had called," Hutch said, "I would've gotten out of the way like I do when Cody or Alex calls me off on a ball between us."

Still Darryl wouldn't drop it.

He said, "You may be the captain of this team. But everybody who plays ball knows who the captain of the infield is. And it's never no second baseman."

"Okay," Mr. Cullen said, "that's enough."

He reached down and handed Darryl his cap, which had gone flying when Darryl and Hutch had gone flying.

"You both sure you're okay?" Hutch and Darryl, looking at him instead of each other, both nodded. "Then we'll talk this out at practice tomorrow," Mr. Cullen said, and started walking Darryl back toward the bench.

Cody went walking toward second base, picked up Hutch's cap, banged it against his leg to get the dirt off it, came back and handed it to him.

"You really okay?" Cody said to Hutch.

"Yeah."

"Let's go home then."

"Yeah," Hutch said again.

Hutch looked down, noticed he still had his glove on, opened the pocket and saw the ball still in it.

"You gotta come up with a Spanish word to describe that catch, dude," Cody said. "Because English ain't gonna do."

"If I ask you a question, will you answer in plain English?" Hutch said.

"Always."

"Did *you* hear him call for the ball?"

Cody looked down.

"Yeah," he said. "We all did."

HUTCH WAS IN THE PAPERS AGAIN. THE *SUN-SENTINEL* THIS TIME, the big paper in Fort Lauderdale.

The Hutchinsons hardly ever saw the *Sun-Sentinel*, even if the paper was sold up in Palm Beach. But somebody had called Hutch's mom first thing in the morning and she'd run over to the 7-Eleven to get it before she had to leave for work.

When she showed it to Hutch, he'd said, "Great."

"Yes," his mom said, "it must be a terrible burden for you sports celebrities, all this media attention."

"Mom, you don't understand."

"Your picture in the paper being a bad thing? You're right. I don't understand."

Hutch turned the sports section over and said, "It's just going to make Darryl hate me even more."

"I seriously doubt that Darryl hates you."

"He's the star of every team he plays on," Hutch said. "And the last couple of games, people have treated me like *I'm* the star."

Connie Hutchinson said, "And that's a bad thing, too?"

"Darryl thinks it was his ball, that it should have been

his catch," Hutch said. "He called for it and everybody heard him except me, and so he blames me for us banging into each other . . . "

He leaned back in his chair so far that he nearly tipped over, and said, "Aw, I give up."

"Talk to Darryl," his mom said. "Even though it's not the guy thing to do."

Hutch didn't care if it was the guy thing to do or not. He knew his mom was right. Hutch decided to make things right with Darryl, even though he hadn't meant to do anything wrong.

After all, it wasn't like he was trying *not* to hear him when they were both going after the ball. Wasn't like he *wanted* to run into the guy at full speed and maybe lose the game in the process. If you thought about it, the only thing Hutch was guilty of was trying *too* hard, concentrating so much on trying to make a play and win the game that he had blocked out everything else.

Including the sound of Darryl's voice.

But none of that mattered now.

It was Hutch's job as team captain—as a team *guy*—not to let things get any worse between him and Darryl, not when they were so close to winning a championship. They had to stop acting like they were on different teams instead of being *teammates.* Hutch wanted to root for Darryl and have Darryl root for him, mostly because he'd never been on a good team in his life when everybody wasn't rooting for everybody else.

So what if Hutch had been on television? So what if he was in the papers again?

Everybody knew this was Darryl's team.

Everybody knew who their star really was.

Didn't they?

• • •

Hutch thought Cody might fight him on apologizing to Darryl, just because Cody had never acted like Darryl's biggest fan. But when Hutch told him on the way to practice what he planned to do, Cody agreed it was a good idea.

"You know why?" Cody said. "Because you don't need the hassle."

"I'm just gonna tell him that if everybody heard him except me, that's on *me*," Hutch said. "It's what a captain should do."

There was a little convenience store a block away from the field, and Mrs. Hester dropped them there, so they could pick up some Gatorade. Before she drove away, she reminded them that Mr. Hutchinson was picking them up today.

They bought two quart bottles of blue Gatorade each, threw them in their bat bags, and walked the rest of the way to Santaluces. They weren't in their spikes yet, just wearing their flip-flops, knowing they were early, not caring. They could never be early enough for baseball. And usually they were the first ones to arrive at practice.

But not today.

Hutch was the one who heard the sound of a ball hitting an aluminum bat, right before he saw that there were already two people on the field at Santaluces, one hitting ground balls, the other fielding them out at short, mimicking throws over to first before lobbing the ball back to home plate.

The fielder was Darryl, who was never early to practice even though he lived only a few blocks from here with his mom. But he was early today.

That wasn't the biggest surprise.

Not even close.

The biggest surprise was the guy at the plate.

Hutch's dad.

CODY SPOKE FIRST, JUST BECAUSE ONE OF THEM HAD TO SAY something.

They were standing behind the black Sun Coast town car that Hutch knew his dad must have driven here, the car hiding them from Carl Hutchinson and Darryl Williams, at least for now.

"Is your dad, like, *lost* or something?"

"Looks right at home, if you ask me."

Cody said, "He barely even comes to *games*."

"Tell me about it."

"So what's he doing out there?" Cody said.

Hutch's dad had jogged out to short now, was crouched in front of Darryl.

Hutch said, "Showing him how to put his glove straight down, then bring it straight up once the ball is in it."

It was one of the first things Hutch could remember his dad teaching him. Before his dad stopped teaching him baseball things. Hutch was seven. His dad had brought a small plywood board out into the yard, told Hutch to pretend the wood was his glove, showed him how to put it straight down on the ground and then use his bare hand to pin the ball against it.

Then he'd shown Hutch how to keep that bare hand on the ball as the board came up, almost like a snatch move, before he set himself to make his throw.

When he was seven, Hutch thought he could practice for a thousand years and not make it look as easy as his dad did.

Hutch remembered everything about that day, remembered how his dad stayed out there until he was satisfied Hutch was doing it the way he'd wanted him to, finally telling him, "This is a hard game. If you're going to learn it, you might as well learn it right."

Then he'd gone back inside the house, telling Hutch that if he wanted to keep practicing, he could throw the ball against the little pitchback he'd bought for him.

Now he was out near second base doing the same thing with Darryl Williams, putting his own glove down in the dirt—where did the glove come from? Hutch wondered, he didn't even know his dad still owned one—and then bringing it up in that old snatch move, making it look as effortless as he always had.

Next he went and stood behind the pitcher's mound, with what had to be Darryl's bat in his hands, rocketing grounders at Darryl from there, unable to get one past him.

Hutch watched them, thinking:

It's like they're the same player.

"You want to go join 'em?" Cody said. "We can't hide here behind this car all afternoon."

"No," Hutch said. "Still looks to me like the two of them are doing just fine on their own."

He could feel heat on the back of his neck, like somebody had just turned up the sun.

How many times? Hutch thought.

How many times had he wanted to be alone on a field, any field, with his dad the way he was alone out there with Darryl Williams right now?

Hutch watched now as his dad walked back to home plate, heard him yell out, "One more."

Coach Carl Hutchinson.

He hit one more rocket. This one was to Darryl's right. Darryl went to his knees, made a sliding stop, whipped a throw across the diamond that would have been dead solid perfect if somebody had been standing on the bag.

"Can't lie to you, son," Carl Hutchinson shouted, flipping the bat over his head as if surrendering. "That's the way I used to pick 'em."

Hutch tried to remember one time in his life when his dad had said anything like that to him, but couldn't.

He and Cody came out from behind the car now, walking toward the home team's bench at Santaluces.

It was then that Carl Hutchinson noticed them.

"Hey," he said, "how long you guys been here?"

Hutch said, "Long enough." He sat down on the bench, made himself very busy putting on his socks and his baseball shoes, as if knotting the laces just right was the most important thing he was going to do all day.

Or all summer.

"Man, I am out of shape," his dad said.

Darryl was with them now, having retrieved the ball

from where it had ended up against the wire fence in back of first.

"Don't believe *that*," Darryl said. "Captain, you never told me you had such a cool dad."

Maybe because I didn't know myself, Hutch thought.

Darryl said, "I can't believe how much I learned in, like, fifteen minutes."

"Yeah," Hutch said, not looking up at either one of them. "My dad sure knows his baseball."

• • •

The way it happened, Carl Hutchinson explained to his son, was this:

He had made an airport run to Fort Lauderdale earlier in the day and was supposed to wait down there and pick up an arriving passenger and drive him to the Ritz-Carlton in Manalapan. But then the arriving passenger's flight was canceled and he knew he had to pick up Hutch and Cody, so he'd decided to surprise Hutch and watch practice for the first time all season.

"Surprise!" Hutch said when he finished, his smile as fake as the one you gave if you got a present you actually hated.

"When I got here," his dad continued, "Darryl was the only one here, and I decided to change in the car and work him out a little bit."

"Whatevs," Hutch said.

A Cody word. One that usually expressed total indifference, not that Hutch's dad was going to pick up on that.

"Darryl had an extra glove with him he's breaking in," his dad said. "That's the way I used to do it. Had one glove as my gamer and another one warming up in the bullpen, in case something happened to the gamer."

"Dad," Hutch said, "I gotta get out there and start warming up."

Like: Sorry to interrupt such a fascinating story.

The rest of the Cardinals were starting to show up now. Hutch saw Tripp and Tommy and Brett, Paul Garner, Hank Harding. He was looking at them, not his dad.

"Everything okay?" his dad said.

"Fine."

"I thought you'd be happier to see me," his dad said.

Yeah, Hutch wanted to say, if you'd shown up about five years ago.

"I'm happy to see you back on the field, Dad," Hutch said, and then jogged toward the outfield to shag balls, just because that was as far away from his dad as he could get right now.

Darryl was at first base, throwing grounders across the diamond to Hank Harding.

"You are so lucky, man," Darryl said to Hutch.

Hutch had no choice but to stop.

"Yeah," he said. "Lucky me."

"Not only do you have a dad," Darryl said, "you've got a *baseball* dad. You never told me your old man almost made it to the majors."

Hutch did not want to have this conversation with him right now, or maybe ever. But there was something in his voice Hutch had never heard before. He didn't know if it was a kind of sadness. Or envy. Something, though. Something that didn't make him sound cool or cocky or better than everybody else. Something that made Hutch want to like him for more than the way he could play baseball.

"I never even *met* my dad," Darryl said. Quietly, almost as if talking to himself instead of to Hutch.

"Sorry," Hutch said, knowing how weak that sounded, truly weak, but knowing it was the best he could do right now.

"My mom says that even if he'd hung around, he wouldn't have been here, y'know?" Darryl said. "What I know of him is just scraps and pieces."

"He like baseball?" Hutch asked.

"Only to bet on it, according to my mom."

Now Hutch really didn't have anything to say, so he just ran out to where Cody was waiting for him in right field.

When he got there, Cody said, "You talk things out with Darryl like you said you were going to?"

"Never got around to it," Hutch said. "He just wanted to tell me what a cool dad I have and how lucky I am."

Cody said, "I know you probably don't want to hear this, but your dad probably didn't think he was doing anything wrong—"

Hutch cut him off. "Yeah, the way he doesn't think he's doing anything wrong when he doesn't even want to *watch* baseball with me, when the only company he seems to want is a stupid can of beer."

"Maybe we should change the subject," Cody said.

"Maybe we should," Hutch said, and then Cody was talking

about tomorrow night's game, about how good he'd heard their opponent, Punta Gorda, was, about last night's Marlins game, about this Web Gem highlight of Ken Griffey Jr. he'd seen on *SportsCenter*, Griffey running into another wall and making another amazing catch and not ending up on the disabled list for once.

Sometimes Cody acted as if he thought talking could fix anything.

Mr. Cullen called everybody in a few minutes later, saying they were going to have batting practice first today, that he wanted the regulars to make a quick run through the order, Tommy O'Neill taking Brett's place behind the plate so Brett could hit, Chris Mahoney calling balls and strikes.

Alex Reyes led off, the way he always did, and when Mr. Cullen buckled his knees on an 0-2 count with a big breaking curve, Mahoney made a big show of punching him out, which drew hoots from the rest of the team.

As Brett dug in, Darryl came and stood next to Hutch.

"The way I've been off the last couple of games with my stroke," Darryl said, "I probably should be asking your dad for batting tips, not fielding tips."

Hutch was swinging two bats, trying to get loose. Trying to make his voice sound loose, casual, he said to Darryl, "Go ahead and ask him if you want, he's sitting right behind us in the bleachers."

"Nah, I don't want to bother him any more today," Darryl said.

"I'm sure it wouldn't be a bother. He seemed to be having a great time with you out there."

"The best," Darryl said. "He must've taught you everything you know."

Hutch couldn't decide whether Darryl was messing with
him or not, so he used a line he'd heard in a movie one time.
"Just not everything *he* knows," Hutch said.

Brett walked on four pitches, Mr. Cullen complaining to
Mahoney about the last two calls.

Hutch's turn at bat now.

He wanted to hit the first good pitch he saw as far as he
had ever hit a baseball. Wanted to feel—and hear—his aluminum bat crush the ball. Wanted to show his dad that Hutch
was pretty good at this game, too.

He knew the biggest mistake a hitter could make was
squeezing the bat and *trying* to hit a home run, that it was
the the surest and quickest way to screw up your swing.

Hutch didn't care.

Not today.

Whatever crazy mixed-up feelings he was carrying with
him to the batter's box right now, he was determined to take
everything out on the ball.

He swung at and missed the first pitch and then took an
even harder swing on the second pitch. Missed that, too. At 0-2,
he took his wildest swing yet, a caveman swing, worse than the
one Darryl had knocked himself down with last night.

He was lucky to get a piece of the ball, off the end of the
bat, grounding weakly down the first-base line.

After Hutch had run it out, Mr. Cullen called over to him,
"Okay, who are you and what have you done with sweet-
swinging Captain Hutchinson?"

"Just trying too hard today, Coach," Hutch said.

Mr. Cullen gave him a funny look and said, "Yeah, I get that. What I'm wondering is, why?"

From the batter's box Darryl said, "Maybe trying to show his dad a little something special." Mocking him.

"No," Hutch said, going to get his glove. "You're dead wrong, as a matter of fact."

"Sure about that?" Darryl said.

It was like Hutch could hear the smile in his voice before he turned and saw it on Darryl Williams' face, Darryl looking first at Hutch, then behind the plate where Carl Hutchinson was sitting, then back at Hutch.

Like he'd figured everything out.

• • •

With about a half hour left in practice, after everybody had gotten their swings in, Mr. Cullen gathered the team around him near the pitcher's mound and talked about what Hutch knew everyone was *thinking* about:

Being one game away from Roger Dean Stadium, from getting their chance to play the state finals on the big field there.

"They said our team was too young," he said, grinning at them. "But that got old fast, didn't it, boys?"

Then he talked about what he had talked about the first day they were together, talked about pitching and defense, saying that in the end, no matter what level of baseball you were talking about, it always came down to pitching and defense for the best teams, with hardly any exceptions.

"So even though you're all tired and thirsty and your minds are already down in Lauderdale getting ready to play the Punta Gorda Pirates tomorrow night, guess what we're going to work on?" Mr. Cullen said. "I mean, since we *know* we got the pitching."

They all knew the answer he was looking for.

"Defense!" they shouted at him.

Behind him Hutch heard Darryl say, "Except D-Will don't want to work on any more dee-fense today."

Hutch knew Mr. Cullen had to have heard, too, but if he did, he didn't let on. He just told the regulars to go take their places on defense. And as Hutch ran out to second, he heard Mr. Cullen call out, "Mr. Hutchinson?"

Hutch stopped, turned around. "Yes, Coach?"

Only Mr. Cullen wasn't talking to him.

"Sorry, I meant Hutch *Senior*," he said, grinning.

Then he yelled up to the stands and said, "I've been waiting all year to have you show up early for one of my practices."

"Why's that?" Hutch's dad yelled back.

"Because I was hoping to get a chance to put you to work," Mr. Cullen said. "You probably have forgotten more about baseball than I know."

Hutch's dad just dismissed that with a wave of his hand.

"Seriously," Mr. Cullen said. "You mind helping out a little today, long as you're here?"

Say no, Hutch said to himself.

"Why not?" his dad said.

He got up, stretched, then made his way down the aluminum bleachers and around the screen behind home plate and out onto the field.

"What do you want me to do?" Carl said.

Mr. Cullen said, "Go out there to second and get with my star middle infielders. Including one I think you know."

"I can do that."

"I'll put some runners in motion from various places," Mr. Cullen said, "set up some situations like we usually do at this time of day. Then you check where Darryl and Hutch are playing, where they're going with the ball. See if an old infielder sees some stuff I don't."

Hutch's dad said, "Got it," and ran out to the back of the infield dirt, giving a little hop over the bag as he did.

Mr. Cullen put Chris Mahoney on first, said Tommy O'Neill would be the runner from home as soon as the ball was in play.

Darryl turned around to Hutch's dad now, and said, "I didn't know there were so many fine points to playing short until you started showing me, Mr. H."

He knows, Hutch thought.

It's why he was smiling at me before. He knows it bothered me seeing him on the field with my dad.

It's why he wants to act like my dad is *his* baseball dad all of a sudden.

They went through various situations for about fifteen minutes. Darryl and Hutch made a couple of double plays, had to go to the outfield a bunch of times to get relay throws—"Was I out far enough, Mr H?" Darryl said one time—and it all would have been a routine ending to practice except for this:

Every time Darryl asked his dad for advice or thanked him for *giving* advice, Hutch felt himself getting madder and madder.

Like a balloon somebody was blowing too much air into, one getting ready to pop.

His dad would give a pointer to Hutch once in a while, too, move him a few feet this way or that, ask him where the ball was going if it was hit to his right or left. But Hutch felt like his dad was just going through the motions, throwing him an occasional bone, that he didn't really care where the second baseman was or what he was doing.

Carl Hutchinson couldn't help himself. He was a shortstop still, focusing on shortstop things, seeing everything through his shortstop's eyes.

It didn't matter that the second baseman was his own kid, because the kid was still nothing more than a second baseman.

With a few minutes to go, Mr. Cullen put Alex, their fastest guy, on first and sent Tripp out to the mound and told him to just lob some pitches in, they were going to try a couple of bunt plays.

Tripp got into his stretch position. Mr. Cullen squared to bunt. When it was clear Tripp was delivering the ball to the plate, not throwing over to first, Alex took off.

"He's going!" Brett yelled.

Then Mr. Cullen, even though he really wanted to lay down a bunt, missed the ball completely.

Alex ran hard from first anyway, making the play into a straight steal.

Usually Hutch would have been moving to cover first on a sacrifice bunt. But as soon as Mr. Cullen missed the pitch, Hutch raced to his right, trying to beat Alex to second base, keeping his eyes on Brett, who'd bounced out from behind the plate and unleashed one of his big throws.

A few feet from the bag, Hutch looked up and saw that Darryl had come over to cover, too.

They didn't run into each other this time, both of them pulling up at the same moment, both of them watching Brett's throw sail into center as Alex raced for third.

Before Darryl could say anything—and Hutch could see he really wanted to—Carl Hutchinson said, "Shortstop covers on that play. Even Little Leaguers know that."

"But—" Hutch started to say.

"No buts about it," his dad snapped. "You should have been moving toward first as soon as Coach showed bunt."

Then he pointed to his head and said, "You gotta think out here."

"Yeah," Darryl said to Hutch, shaking his head, walking back toward short. "Think like a second baseman."

And that was it. The balloon finally burst.

Hutch followed him.

"Maybe I get crossed up sometimes," Hutch yelled, "because I've gotten used to doing the thinking for both of us. Even though you want my dad to think you're more interested in defense than Ozzie Smith all of a sudden."

Darryl turned and smiled another one of his smiles.

"That's not what's making you hot, though, is it, Hutch *Junior*?" Darryl said.

"What's that supposed to mean?" Hutch said, still yelling at him, in a voice he barely recognized as his own.

When Darryl answered, it was in a voice only loud enough for Hutch to hear.

He said, "What's the matter, Hutch *Junior*? You afraid your daddy likes me better than you?"

Hutch didn't say anything, didn't think, just dropped his glove and went after him, put his head down and drove his shoulder into Darryl's stomach like this was football, put him down as hard as he could.

By the time the two of them had been pulled apart, Hutch had been suspended from the Punta Gorda game.

THEY WERE IN THE FRONT SEAT OF THE COMPANY CAR. HUTCH'S dad had the key in the ignition but still hadn't started the engine. The two of them just sat there in the new parking lot at Santaluces.

Talking to each other about as much as they usually did.

Finally Carl Hutchinson said, "I ought to make you sit in the backseat."

Hutch just sat there in silence.

His dad said, "Want to know why?"

"Why?"

"Because right now I feel like I don't know you any better than the people I drive around in this thing, that's why."

"Maybe you don't," Hutch said.

Now his dad put the car in gear, pulled out onto Hypoluxo, drove them past the 7-Eleven where Hutch and Cody had stopped for Gatorade, back when the only problem in Hutch's life was what he was going to say to Darryl Williams when he tried to make things right between them.

Good job with that, Hutch thought now.

Cody had gone home with Mr. Cullen, the coach saying it

was right on his way, telling Hutch's dad, "I have a feeling you and your boy have some things to talk about."

Hutch hadn't thrown any punches at Darryl once they were on the ground, but then he'd never had the urge to punch him. It wasn't about that. He just needed to put him down in the heat of that moment, knock that smirk out of his voice and off his face.

Hutch knew, in the smart part of his brain, the part he wasn't using, how stupid this whole thing was—"juvenile" was the word his mom always used for dumb guy things—but he still couldn't have stopped himself. He knew Darryl had tried to get under his skin, knew what was happening between them was sillier than the silliest beef on a playground, one guy saying your dad liked him better.

Didn't matter.

He went for Darryl the way you went for a high fastball you knew you should lay off sometimes, no matter how much you told yourself it was a sucker pitch.

It had taken half the team to get them separated. Brett took hold of Darryl, while Carl Hutchinson had his long arms around Hutch.

Darryl wasn't smirking now, wasn't wearing that smile any longer, just pointed a finger at Hutch and said, "That's your *one*."

"One what?" Hutch said.

"One free shot," Darryl said. "Next one's mine."

"There isn't going to be a next one, for either one of you!" Mr. Cullen had yelled. "This ends here and it ends *now*. Is that understood?"

Hutch and Darryl weren't looking at him, they were still looking at each other, still trying to stare each other down. Playground stuff to the end.

"I didn't do anything," Darryl said.

"Right," Hutch said.

"Am . . . I . . . understood?" Mr. Cullen said, spitting out the words one at a time.

Reluctantly, both Hutch and Darryl nodded.

It was then that Mr. Cullen had turned to Hutch and said, "What were you *possibly* thinking?"

And Hutch Hutchinson, who had just shown he didn't have the best judgment in the world, but who still prided himself on telling the truth, told the truth now.

"I wasn't thinking."

Mr. Cullen shook his head, exasperated, took off his Cardinals cap the way he would sometimes after they got a bad call, and ran his hand through what hair he had left.

It was then that his coach hit Hutch a lot harder than Hutch had hit Darryl.

"You're out of the game tomorrow night," he said. "I love most everything about you, Hutch. Love your game, love your passion for the game, love your heart. But I wouldn't let another player on this team get away with what you just did, and I'm not gonna let you get away with it, even if it costs you—and us—our season. Now is *that* understood?"

"Yes, sir," Hutch said.

They had all stood there for what felt like an hour to Hutch, Mr. Cullen done now, nobody on the team saying anything, until Hutch's dad had said, "Let's go."

Now they were in the car, this quiet car that was much nicer than their own Camry, Carl Hutchinson gripping the steering wheel with those big baseball hands of his.

"Why?" he said to Hutch.

"I don't want to talk about it."

"You can decide something like that, whether you want to talk about it, when you're the dad someday. But I'm the dad here. So you're sure-as-Sunday gonna talk about it now."

Hutch slouched down even lower in the passenger seat than he already was. Where did he even start a conversation like the one his dad wanted to have now?

When he was seven?

Hutch thought of himself as a pretty smart guy. Not the smartest kid in his class. But smart enough. Just not right now. How did he explain to his dad, how did he make him understand that he'd been waiting for his dad to come out and play with him for the past five years . . . that when he finally came out of the house to play ball, even for a few minutes, he'd done it with Darryl?

"How come you want to start talking to me now?" Hutch said.

"That's a question, not an answer."

"It'll have to do."

"Don't use that snippy tone of voice on me," his dad said. "I didn't do anything tonight."

"Who are you, Darryl?"

"I'm your father," Carl Hutchinson said, "the one who's trying to understand why you'd do something to hurt your team that way."

"I wasn't trying to hurt my team," Hutch said. "I was just tired of him mouthing off."

"Mouthing off about what?" his dad said. "I was out there and I didn't hear anything."

"Dad, you only hear what you want to hear most of the time."

"We're back to me again?"

"Anyway, what matters is that I heard him," Hutch said.

"And what did you hear that was so terrible that you had to go after him like one of those soccer nuts in the World Cup?"

"Why don't you ask him the next time you're giving him a private baseball lesson?"

The words just came out of Hutch, nothing he could do to stop them. It would have been like trying to stop a wave off Boynton Beach.

They were at a stoplight.

Carl Hutchinson turned to his son.

"Is *that* what this is about?"

Hutch turned and looked at him.

Another staredown, with his dad this time, not feeling so different from the one he'd had with Darryl.

"Yeah," he said to his dad. "I guess it is."

• • •

After that Hutch just let it rip.

About how it should have been him on that field, not Darryl, how Darryl could never have shown him up as much as his own dad had today, acting like he cared more about Darryl than he did about his own son.

He was shouting and his dad wasn't stopping him.

"I can't even remember the last time you were out on a field with me, acted like you *wanted* to be out on a field with me, if I *tried!*" Hutch said.

He turned away, feeling like his heart was going as fast as the car, noticing for the first time that they were on the Florida Turnpike for some reason. Wondering where in the world they were headed.

His dad gave him a quick sideways glance. "Can *I* say something about your friend Darryl before you start in on him again?"

"He's *not* my friend!" Hutch said. "Why can't you get that? He never wanted to *be* my friend. He didn't want me to be captain, he doesn't act like he even wants to be on the same team with me. The other day, he went out of his way to get me run over on a stupid routine force play."

"He did what?"

"Never mind."

They were in the left lane, going at a pretty good clip. But then his dad always said that the Florida Turnpike was like the Daytona 500, just with amateurs.

Now his dad said, "You're dead wrong about what happened tonight. It didn't mean anything. Least not to me."

"Well it did to *me*," Hutch said. "And don't tell me it didn't mean anything to you. I could see you were having big fun out there. So could Cody."

"I got no reason to lie to you, son," Carl Hutchinson said.

"All I was doing was killing time." His voice was the total opposite of Hutch's, barely louder than the sound of the engine from the Sun Coast company car. "That's all baseball ever is to me now. A way to kill time."

He slowed the car down now, got back in the right lane, put on his right blinker, and took the Okeechobee exit off the Turnpike.

"Great, Dad," Hutch said. "So you're saying you don't even care about *my* baseball now. Sorry you have to kill so much time coming to watch my games." Hutch paused and then said, "Why do you ever bother showing up for my games, anyway?"

"That's not what I'm saying."

Hutch clenched his fists, pounded them on his knees. "Then what are you saying?"

"I'm saying that when it comes to baseball, I don't let myself care too much, not even about you," Carl Hutchinson said. "*Especially* about you."

"Well, I want you to care!" Hutch was yelling again. "*I care, don't you get that?*"

"Looked tonight like you cared a little too much," his dad said.

He paid the toll now, went through the booth, took a right on Okeechobee Boulevard.

"You cared so much," Carl Hutchinson continued, "that you acted like you'd lost your stinkin' mind and cost yourself a chance to play in a championship game. And guess what, son? You don't know how many games like that you're gonna get in your life, trust me on that."

Hutch was still stuck about his dad not caring, couldn't make himself move off that.

He said to his dad, "You sure looked like you cared about baseball with Darryl when you were showing him that old board drill of yours."

"That's the thing," his dad said, "what I'm trying to explain to you, even if I'm not doing a very good job of it."

"*What* thing?"

They were taking another right, into what looked like some kind of big complex for condominiums. Hutch had barely noticed how fast it had gotten dark since they'd left Santaluces.

"It costs me nothing, working with a guy like Darryl," his dad said in that quiet voice of his, the one that made Hutch think sometimes he went through life talking like people did in the library. "Because he *doesn't* care."

"How can you be as good as he is, as *great* as he is, and not care?" Hutch said.

"Oh, he cares, all right," Carl Hutchinson said. "Just not like you. He loves baseball for what it's gonna do for him someday, because he's sure it's gonna make him rich and famous and get his momma out of Lantana and all like that." He nodded and said, "All the things I was gonna do when I was his age. He just doesn't love baseball for baseball. The way you love it."

Hutch thought about the Hun School of Princeton, New Jersey, pictured the cover of that brochure he kept hidden in his room.

But he wasn't going to tell his dad about it, not tonight, not until he absolutely had to.

He just felt tired all of a sudden. "It still should have been me out there with you. If you wanted to get back on the field, why couldn't it be with me?"

It was then that he noticed the sign for the Emerald Dunes Golf Club.

Hutch looked at that, then looked at his dad, saw that his dad was the one who really looked tired now, looked as tired and beaten as he ever had.

"You want to know where you end up if you care too much about baseball?" Carl Hutchinson said. *"Here."*

HUTCH HAD NEVER BEEN HERE. AND DIDN'T WANT TO BE HERE now. He just wanted to go home, go to his room, get grounded or whatever his dad was going to put on top of the suspension Mr. Cullen had given him, get a little bit closer to this day being over.

But he could see that wasn't happening anytime soon.

"Dad," Hutch said, "I don't want to do this tonight."

"I do," he said. "Now get out of the car."

There were still some outside lights on at Emerald Dunes, even though his dad said everybody who worked here had gone home by now. His dad showed him where the caddies changed, showed him the construction they were still doing on the new clubhouse, took him around back and showed him where the new dining room was going to be, overlooking the 18th green.

It looked like a nice place to Hutch, but he knew he wasn't here so his dad could show off Emerald Dunes to him. Maybe in this way, Hutch and his dad weren't so different. Hutch had never asked his dad any questions about this place, had shown about as much of an interest in his dad's day job as his dad showed in Hutch's baseball.

But this wasn't the night to talk about that, to try and explain to his dad that he didn't want to know about Emerald Dunes or what his dad did here because he didn't want to think of him in those white overalls.

"'Bout time you saw your dad's real office," he said. "Sometimes when I want to clear my head at night, I get into the car and drive over here and walk around like this by myself."

So that's where he goes, Hutch thought.

But how could you find peace at night at the same place where you had to carry around guys' golf bags during the day?

There was, Hutch decided, even more he didn't know about his dad than he'd ever imagined.

Then they were walking past the practice putting green and around to their right, where Hutch's dad said the first tee was, walking on the cart path past that tee, walking in the direction of Okeechobee Boulevard.

Another silence between them.

Neither one of them saying anything about Darryl or baseball or fathers or sons.

It was weird, Hutch thought. All the times when he'd wanted his dad to talk with him, about anything, and now he was happy to find himself in another one of their silences.

Until his dad finally said:

"It wasn't my shoulder."

Hutch couldn't see his face.

"What?"

"Your whole life, I let you think that I really started washing out of the minor leagues because I hurt my throwing shoulder," he said. "That I couldn't make the throw from the hole after that, that it screwed up my swing. But that was just a lie I came up with."

Hutch said, "I don't understand."

His dad said, "It was just a way of me not admitting to people what I'd already admitted to myself *before* I got hurt."

Hutch nearly tripped over something in the dark.

"Drain pipe," his dad said. "You know who tore up his knee bad because of a drain pipe?"

"Mickey Mantle," Hutch said. "He was playing right because Joe DiMaggio was still in center, even though he was much older than Mantle. DiMaggio called him off on a ball and Mantle pulled up, but he got his spikes caught on an outfield drain. Messed up his knee bad."

"Why am I not surprised you know that?"

They kept walking toward Okeechobee, the car lights up ahead of them, his dad pointing toward a lit-up office building in the distance that he said belonged to Homeland Security.

"I wasn't good enough," his dad said. "Oh, I was the best to ever come out of East Boynton Little League and Boynton Beach High, the way a lot of other guys in the minors are the best guy from someplace. And I sure did believe what people told me about where I was going in baseball. You always do that when people promise you your dream is gonna come true. And I was like you. I wanted it more than anything. Wanted it because I loved the game like it was my whole life."

In Hutch's whole life, he had never heard his dad say that the two of them were alike.

Hutch wondered if they were going to walk all 18 holes of the golf course, like his dad planned to do a whole loop, which is what he called carrying somebody's bag the whole 18.

"This is my long-winded way of saying I don't want to happen to you what happened to me," Carl Hutchinson said.

"It won't," Hutch said.

"It broke me when I found out I wasn't good enough, that I wasn't really as good as everybody *said* I was. Nobody can prepare you for that, having your dreams killed," his dad said. "Now I see you making the same mistake I made. Wanting it too much."

Hutch stopped now.

"How could you possibly know that?" he said.

"Know what?"

"How could you possibly know how much I want anything?"

"You're my son. I can see myself in you."

"Then how come you never told me that before tonight?" Hutch felt himself getting mad all over again, and didn't care, not even a little bit. His father had brought him here and wanted to talk and they were going to talk. "The problem is, you never took the time to know me, Dad. You've never asked me about my dreams one single time."

"You want to be a ballplayer," his dad said. "You've always wanted to be a ballplayer, and I could see from the start there was nothing I could do to stop you."

"So *that's* your excuse for ignoring me?" Hutch said.

"That was your way of trying to *help* me? Do you have any idea how weak that is?"

"Don't talk to me that way," his dad said, getting hot himself now.

"Sorry if I don't know how to talk to you, Dad, but let's face it, it's not like I've had a lot of practice."

It was on now between them, *so* on, no stopping it. This probably wasn't the heart-to-heart, the father-son talk, his dad had planned. But this was the one they were having now, standing out here on the golf course in the night.

Hutch said, "Are you trying to tell me you hardly ever coached me because you didn't want me to care too much? How about giving *me* a vote on that? How about asking me what *I* thought? All the times I wanted to play ball with you so much and I couldn't, and it was like somebody punched me right in the gut . . ."

He stopped because he was afraid if he didn't, he might start crying.

"Don't," his dad said.

"Don't what?" Hutch said. "Tell you the truth? You know what I think the truth really is, Dad? That you don't want me to care so much about baseball because you don't think I'm good enough. Not as good as you were when you were my age."

On the empty golf course, wherever they were on the No. 1 hole, Hutch's words came out so loud, it was like they were booming out of a PA system at the ballpark.

"That's not what I mean."

"You never wanted to help me before," Hutch said. "So don't start helping me now."

Then before his dad could say anything back, Hutch said: "It doesn't matter, anyway, because I'm leaving."

"What does that mean?"

"You know what my *real* dream is, Dad?" Hutch said. "To get a baseball scholarship up north someplace and get out of here the first chance I get."

"You never said anything about that," his dad said.

"One more thing you didn't ask me about," Hutch said.

He left his dad standing there, walked away from Okeechobee, pretty sure he was going the right way, toward the parking lot, saying over his shoulder, "Please take me home now."

Nothing more to say.

For either one of them.

He told his mom about the fight with Darryl as soon as he got home, just because he knew he was going to have to tell her sooner or later.

Hutch hoped his dad wouldn't stay in the room, so he could tell it his own way. But his dad sat right next to her on the couch in the living room, showing about as much expression as he did when he was on that couch watching baseball by himself.

When Hutch was done, Connie Hutchinson looked at her husband and said, "It happened that way?"

"Pretty much. I didn't hear what Darryl said to him right before. Our boy acted like an idiot after that, but he doesn't lie."

"I see," was all she said.

"Can I go?" Hutch said.

What had officially become the longest night of his life wasn't over yet.

"Not quite yet," she said. She turned to her husband and said, "So what do we do about this, other than telling him nothing like it had better happen again?"

"Nothing," his dad said. "Nothing could be a worse

punishment than his missing that game tomorrow night. I don't know a lot. But I know that."

"No grounding then?"

"If his team loses and it's even partly because he's not there, it'll be the worst grounding he's ever gotten. Because he'll have grounded himself from baseball for the rest of his summer."

He wanted to defend himself, wanted to tell both his parents that he never lost his temper like this, never got into this kind of trouble. He'd never even gotten grounded before.

But all he said was, "We're not going to lose."

Like he was trying to convince himself of that more than his mom and dad.

"It would be a shame if you did," his mom said. "But it would teach you a valuable lesson, Keith."

"Keith" was never good. Keith meant *she* meant business.

"*Keith*," his dad said, making it almost sarcastic, making it sound like Darryl calling him "Captain," "is lucky he didn't get kicked off the team."

His dad didn't mention boarding school nor the trip to Emerald Dunes, and neither did Hutch, not even when Hutch's mom asked them why they were so late. His dad just said, "We drove around a bit and talked," and left it at that.

"Can I please go to my room now?" Hutch said.

"Fine with me," his dad said. "I've got nothing more to say, anyway."

He got up and walked out of the room. When he was gone, Connie Hutchinson leaned forward and said in a soft voice, "I'm sorry."

"Me, too."

"You don't know what I'm sorry about."

"Mom, can't we just call it a night?"

"I'm sorry it hurt you so much, seeing your dad on that field with Darryl."

"I'll get over it."

He went upstairs, closed the door, turned on his dinky fan, flopped on the bed. He tried to close his eyes, but as soon as he did, he saw himself charging Darryl again. So he got up, got out one of his favorite DVDs, the Yankees highlight DVD from the 2001 postseason. He sat down at his desk, turned on his laptop, the used Dell they'd bought for him, inserted the disk, and found the flip play Jeter had made against the A's.

Hutch watched it over and over.

Watched Jeter be in the right place, make the right decision, again and again and again, on the night when Hutch had made the dumbest decision on a ball field he'd ever made in his life.

When he finally got tired of watching, he got back on his bed, stared at the shadows on his ceiling, and tried to imagine something that would make Jeter charge A-Rod the way he had charged Darryl tonight.

But he couldn't.

● ● ●

"You're coming to the game," Cody said to Hutch, "even if I have to tie you up like they do in the movies and throw you in the trunk of the car."

"It's a bus, Codes."

"I'm just trying to make a point here."

"And I'm not going," Hutch said.

They had been riding their bikes around the neighborhood for the last hour, making this big loop around the edges
of the world they'd grown up in. They rode up and down
Seacrest for a while, past some houses whose windows were
still boarded up because of the hurricane last year, past an
apartment complex called the Village Royal Green, got passed
a couple of times by a Citizens Observer Patrol Car. When
they reached the Community Center, a couple of blocks south
of Gateway and Seacrest, they turned around and headed for
Cody's house.

Cody liked to call rides like this the *Tour de Hester*.

Every time Hutch would start to think Cody had dropped
the subject of him traveling down to Fort Lauderdale with the
team for the Punta Gorda game, he would bring it up again.

"If I buy the burgers for lunch, will you let this go?" Hutch
said.

"No."

"Burgers *and* ice cream later?"

"I can't be bought."

"Sure you can."

"Good point," Cody said. "Just not today. Today my job is
to be the captain of you, and make you see that as the captain
of the team you should be with us."

"I'm not part of the team today."

"You'd come if you were hurt," Cody said.

"But I'm not hurt," Hutch said. "My dad was right about one thing: The only thing I did last night was hurt you guys."

"Please come," Cody said. "I'm asking you as your best friend."

"Don't," Hutch said.

"You'll figure out a way to help us even from the bench. I know you."

Hutch said, "And *I* know it will kill me having to watch from the bench."

Truth was, it was killing Hutch already just thinking about the game. And he knew it was going to kill him even more tonight, whether he was there or not. When he had finally gone to sleep last night, he had told himself he would feel better about things in the morning. Isn't that what your parents always told you, that everything would look better after a good night's sleep?

They were wrong.

When Hutch woke up and started thinking all over again about what he'd done, he'd only felt worse.

About everything.

He'd let everybody down, no matter how much Cody was trying to prop him back up.

They went back to Cody's house when they were finally tired of riding around, sat down in what shade there was on the Hesters' front porch. Almost noon now, straight up. Four and a half hours until the Cardinals' bus left from Santaluces.

Great, Hutch thought.

Now the longest night of Hutch's life was turning into the longest day.

"What will you do if you don't go?" Cody said.

"Go to bed early and pull the covers over my head until you call and tell me we won."

"I sleep in that room all the time, remember?" Cody said. "You'd suffocate."

Mrs. Hester had the day off from her nursing job. She brought them out glasses of lemonade and said, "Looks to me like I'm interrupting some deep conversation, am I right?"

"No," Hutch said, at the same time Cody said, "Yes."

Mrs. Hester laughed and said, "Wait a second, I thought the two of you were always on the same page."

"Not today," Cody said.

When she was gone, Hutch said, "You've got a cool mom."

"This isn't *Jeopardy!*" Cody said. "Don't try to change the category."

Hutch put his glass down so hard, he was afraid he might have broken it for a second. "We either stop talking about this, or I'm out of here," he said, the words coming out with more snap than he'd intended.

Cody stood up now, face red, a shade he liked to call "redneck red." He said, "You know what? Nobody's stopping you. And if you want to be as selfish today as you were last night, I'm not going to stop you from doing that, either! You want to stay home tonight? Stay. You want to go home and feel sorry for yourself there instead of doing it with me? Go."

It took a lot to get Cody mad, and he hardly ever got mad at Hutch unless it was fake-mad over a video game.

But he was mad now.

"Who is it that's always saying how seriously he takes being captain of the team? Oh, wait: That would be you, wouldn't it? Well, excuse me for thinking you were going to suck it up and be a real captain tonight. You know why we're still talking about this? Because I never thought you'd act like this much of a baby, while the rest of us go down there and try to save your sorry butt."

Hutch sat there and took it from his best friend, staring up at him from the top step.

"So what's it gonna be?" Cody said. "Are you in or are you out?"

Hutch stood up then, so they were eye to eye.

Then he put out his hand for the kind of regulation handshake they only gave themselves when they were shaking on something important.

And this was important.

"I'm in," Hutch said.

He knew he was going to feel like an outsider. But Cody Hester, his redneck friend with the red face, was right. Righter than he knew.

You were either the captain of the team, or you weren't.

Hutch was.

MR. CULLEN WAS STANDING BY THE DOOR TO THE BUS WHEN Mrs. Hester dropped off Hutch and Cody. "I'm glad you came, Hutch."

"I'm sorry again about last night, Mr. C. I've never done anything like that before in my life."

"Last night was last night," Mr. Cullen said. "If there's one thing I've learned in sports, it's that you can't do anything about last night. Lord knows I used to try when I was a player. Let's just do our best to support the guys tonight."

"I'll do whatever you say," Hutch said.

"How about I make you bench coach for a night? You can sit next to me when we're at bat and hold things down when I'm coaching first."

"Cool," Hutch said.

Only he didn't feel very cool.

Other than when he'd sprained an ankle in Little League, he couldn't remember one time in his life when a team of his had a game and he wasn't playing in it.

There was something else bothering him.

He knew he was going to have to talk to Darryl sooner or

later. Not just about what had happened last night, but all the junk that had been going on between them the whole season. Maybe if he'd had the talk last night, the way he'd planned before he showed up for practice and saw his dad on the field, he wouldn't be in the fix he was in now.

Hutch and Cody had grabbed two seats in the very back of the bus by the time Darryl got on. Usually Darryl liked to sit by himself in the back so he could take a nap, no matter how short the trip was. But when he looked up and saw Hutch back there, he sat down in the first row, across from Mr. Cullen, who always had the first seat behind the driver.

The conversation with Darryl would have to be later.

● ● ●

Hutch waited until the Cardinals were about to go out for in-field practice, then walked over to where Darryl was standing at the end of their bench.

"I was out of line last night," he said.

Darryl looked at him, no expression on his face, not mad, not interested, not anything, almost like Hutch was a stranger, before saying, "You *think*?"

"Darryl, we gotta get past this, you and me," Hutch said, keeping his voice low. "For the good of the team."

"You shoulda thought about the good of the team before you sucker-slammed me."

He wasn't going to make it easy.

But why should he? Hutch thought.

I don't deserve it.

And it wasn't like he was going to stop being Darryl just because Hutch had apologized.

Connie Hutchinson liked to say that if you were born round, you didn't die square.

"You're right," Hutch said. He didn't like saying that to Darryl, but he did anyway, swallowing hard like he'd just taken medicine. "I'm just asking you as best I can to go out there tonight and get me a chance to play a few more games this season."

He put out his hand then, but Darryl picked that moment to start fiddling with the straps hanging off his glove.

Leaving Hutch hanging until he just dropped his hand back down to his side.

"Won't be doing it for you," Darryl said.

"I just don't want there to be any more trouble between us, is all," Hutch said.

"That would be up to you, wouldn't it?" Darryl said.

Then the Cardinals shortstop ran out to short, Hutch envying him more than he ever had, just because he had a game to play and Hutch didn't.

● ● ●

The Cardinals were going with their best tonight, which meant Tripp was starting. Cody had replaced Hutch at second, going back to his normal position, and Tommy O'Neill was playing right.

When Mr. Cullen gathered them around him before the

134

game, he announced that he wasn't going to wear anybody out with one of his big rousing pep talks.

"Rousing, Coach?" Cody said.

"Hush and listen," Mr. Cullen said. "Because I've basically got just two words for you tonight: Roger Dean."

Hutch hadn't worn his uniform, even though Cody had tried to get him to. He was wearing shorts and a T-shirt and his favorite sneaks, an old beat-up pair of Nike Franchise Lows. As Mr. Cullen spoke, he hung back behind the guys who were in uniform.

He wasn't a player tonight and wasn't going to pretend like he was, even now.

"When we get back on that bus and go back up 95 tonight," Mr. Cullen said, "we're not just gonna be heading home. We're gonna be on our way to the finals."

He looked from face to face and said, "Are you all hearing me on that?"

"Yes!"

"Then go win the game," he said, and the Cardinals ran out to their positions from the third-base side of the field. Hutch watched them go and felt like he was watching everybody get dismissed from class early except him.

Mr. Cullen must have been watching him watch his teammates, because he put an arm around Hutch's shoulder.

"You want to chart pitches?" he said to Hutch.

"Nah. I can't follow the game doing that, Mr. C. I don't even keep score when I go to Marlins games."

He sat down at the end of the bench and Mr. Cullen sat down next to him.

"So just hang with me, then," Mr. Cullen said. "I watch you when you're playing. I see you moving guys around when you don't think I notice. I know you see stuff in games that nobody else on the team sees."

"I just want to see us *win*," Hutch said.

Tripp threw strike one then to start the game.

"All right!" Hutch yelled.

Mr. Cullen grinned.

"Easy there, tiger."

For some reason Hutch remembered the night they'd all sat in his living room and watched the replay of his home run on television, Cody complaining that Hutch's mom was calling him a cheerleader.

Now Hutch was the cheerleader, at least for a night.

● ● ●

In the fourth inning, the Pirates leading 3–2, Hutch caught Cody's eye when he saw him shading too much toward first with a left-handed hitter, the Pirates catcher, at the plate.

But even though the Pirates had four lefties in their order, only one of them had managed to pull the ball off Tripp so far. Now they had second and third, two out, the catcher up. A base hit was going to put them up by two runs, and Hutch, in his mind's eye, saw that base hit going right up the middle between Cody and Darryl.

So without making a big show of it, any more than he would have made a big show of it on the field, Hutch just hooked a thumb at Cody and told him to move back toward second base.

Cody took two steps.

Hutch motioned with his head for him to keep going.

Cody gave him an are-you-crazy? look, but did what he was told.

When Hutch finally told him to stop, Cody pointed toward the big hole that had opened up between him and Chris Mahoney, playing first with Tripp pitching.

Hutch grinned and made a calming motion with his hands, as if telling him everything was cool.

Mr. Cullen had gone to get a bottle of water out of their cooler, came back with the count 2-2 on the catcher, said to Hutch, "Uh, why is Cody practically standing on second base all of a sudden?"

He started to get up and move him back, but Hutch put a hand on his arm and said, "I told him to play there."

"Guy's a lefty."

"I know, Mr. C," Hutch said. "But you gotta trust your bench coach on this one."

Mr. Cullen took a swig of water, spit it out, and said to Hutch, "You better be right."

Two pitches later the kid at the plate hit a hard grounder up the middle, just to the second baseman's side of the base.

Cody barely had to move.

He was all over the ball, not even having to backhand it, gloving it straight up and having plenty of time to get the out at first and get them out of the inning.

"Oh," Mr. Cullen said, "I get it, *that* was the hole I should have been worrying about."

"No biggie," Hutch said, smiling to himself, feeling for a moment like he was actually in the game.

It was still 3–2, Pirates. The Cardinals had gotten their runs when D-Will had doubled home Alex and Brett in the bottom of the first off the Pirates' lefty starter.

Hutch knew it should have been him bringing the runners around, could have been him if he hadn't acted like such an idiot. But there had been nothing to do back in the first inning except stand and cheer for Darryl like everybody else on the bench.

Tripp, working on a high pitch count, somehow made it through the top of the fifth without giving up another run. The Pirates' starter, who seemed to match every pitch Tripp threw out of the strike zone, walking a half-dozen guys by Hutch's count, only made it through the fourth before the Pirates' manager brought in a big righty who looked like he ought to be playing middle linebacker in football.

Not good.

Not even close.

Because as soon as he'd pitched to his first two Cardinals batters—Chris and Hank—Hutch knew this kid had better stuff than the Pirates' starter—better command, two fastballs, one a riser, the other a mean sinker.

The big righty, a seventeen-year-old for sure, kept the Pirates ahead by a run into the eighth. It was pretty clear to Hutch by then that they were going to pitch him the rest of the way. There wasn't anybody warming up and the kid seemed to be on cruise control, even when the Cardinals would manage to work the count on him a little bit, which wasn't often. The Cardinals were barely forcing him to break a sweat.

"Got any brilliant strategy you're working on?" Cody had said when the Cardinals came in to bat in the bottom of the seventh.

"Yeah," Hutch said. "Score two more runs before that guy gets nine more outs."

"The math sounds simple enough," Cody said.

But the Cardinals managed only a single base runner in the seventh, who was immediately erased when Chris Mahoney hit into a double play.

Chris tried to make up for that by at least pitching a 1-2-3 top of the eighth.

Six more outs for the Cardinals to get those two runs and a trip to Roger Dean.

"I don't know if we can hit this kid," Mr. Cullen said before running out to coach first, just loud enough for Hutch to hear.

Hutch said, "But he *is* hittable, Coach, that's the thing. We're just not being patient enough, making him work hard enough. We're getting ourselves out."

Cody was leading off for them in the bottom of the eighth.

Hutch grabbed him as he was putting on his batting gloves and said, "A walk wouldn't stink here, you know."

"I hear you."

Hutch gave his arm a good squeeze.

"Ow?" Cody said.

Hutch said, "A walk *really* wouldn't stink here."

"Do you think I'm thick or something?" Cody said, then quickly added, "Wait, don't answer that."

Somehow Cody the free swinger worked the count to 3-2. He stepped out for a moment, turned around, caught Hutch's eye, grinned. Then he got back into the box and maybe for the first time in his entire life laid off one of those in-your-eyes fastballs he loved more than chocolate ice cream, and the Pirates' big righty issued his first walk since he'd come into the game.

"Yes!" Hutch said.

Alex Reyes up next, top of the order. He tried to bunt for a base hit and nearly beat it out, the third baseman's throw getting him by a step. Cody moved to second on the play. Not good enough, Hutch thought. Somebody needs to smack one off this kid. He'd had things pretty much his way for four innings now.

If somebody didn't hit a ball hard, and soon, they were going to lose.

Brett was up now. He grounded one that somehow was a foot to the left of the third baseman's glove and a foot to the right of the shortstop's glove, and made it into short left. It looked like Cody might have a chance to score, but the third-base coach wisely held him up at third.

First and third, still one out.

Darryl at the plate, batting third tonight with Hutch not in the lineup.

Only problem? Darryl had done nothing against this

pitcher his first two times up against him, acting as impatient as everybody else, popping out on first pitch, high fastballs both times. It had driven Hutch crazy from the bench.

It was why he'd practically begged Cody to go up there looking for a walk.

But D-Will wasn't going to be looking for a walk here—he was going to be swinging away, looking to be a hero.

He and Hutch hadn't said a word to each other since they'd talked before infield, somehow managing to avoid each other in the bench area all night long. But when the Punta Gorda coach called time-out and jogged out to the mound, probably to tell his pitcher to be careful with Darryl whether he'd popped him up twice or not, Hutch got off the bench and walked toward the on-deck circle.

When he was halfway there, Darryl said to him, "Not now."

Hutch remembered Tim McCarver talking one time on TV about how when he had been catching for the real Cardinals, Bob Gibson would try to glare him away from the mound when McCarver would want to talk to him, but how if McCarver had something important to say, he'd suck it up and keep going.

Hutch kept going.

"Seriously? This is not the time to mess with me," Darryl said.

"I'm not messing with you," Hutch said. "I'm trying to help you."

"Then go sit your butt down. I told you before: Go captain somebody else."

Hutch stood his ground, kept his voice low, and said,

"Just listen to me for one minute. This guy's sequence is exactly the same when one of our guys works the count: high fastball, sinking fastball, change, high fastball again. Every single time. Nobody expects the change because they're fixed on catching up with his high heat."

The Punta Gorda manager was jogging back to the bench.

Darryl said, "And this matters to me *because* . . . ?"

"Because the change just sits there, that's why. He only throws it to set up the next fastball, make it look like it's coming in about a thousand miles an hour."

Darryl wasn't saying anything now.

Or maybe he was actually listening to what Hutch was trying to tell him.

Hutch leaned forward, whispering now. "The change is your mattress ball, dude."

• • •

This time Darryl took the first pitch.

For strike one.

The second fastball was the sinking one, the kind of pitch that always looks like a fat one until it dives toward the catcher's mitt, or the dirt, like a seagull looking for food. Most of the time the big righty had thrown it in the dirt.

This time there was hardly any late break.

Darryl took it. Strike two.

0–2.

He stepped out of the box, messed with his batting gloves

142

for a second, turned and tried to stare a hole right through Hutch.

Hutch didn't move a muscle.

Please, he thought to himself.

Please don't change your sequence now.

The Pirates pitcher went into his stretch, checked Cody at third, looked over his shoulder at Brett taking a short lead off first.

Then he threw his changeup.

Threw his do-nothing changeup and watched Darryl Williams put that effortless swing of his on it, heard the same sound everybody else heard, the sound of the fat part of the bat on a ball that was just about the sweetest sound in this world.

He knew and Darryl knew and everybody in the park knew.

This time when Darryl stopped to watch a few feet out of the batter's box, he had a home run to look at.

To dead center.

No-doubter all the way.

Cardinals 5, Pirates 3.

It ended that way because Pedro Mota struck out the side in the ninth.

When the Pirates' leadoff man swung through strike three for the final out of the game, Hutch led the charge toward the pitcher's mound, trying to get there first, even before Brett made it there from behind the plate.

But Darryl cut him off.

For a second they just stood there in the middle of

the infield, third-base side of the mound, like it was one more staredown between them, neither one of them saying anything.

Until Darryl said, "Good call."

"Better swing," Hutch said.

"Doesn't change things between us," Darryl said. "Just so's you know."

"Didn't expect it to," Hutch said.

When Hutch woke up the next morning, it felt like the first day of summer all over again.

He wanted to play some ball, even though Mr. Cullen had given everybody the day off.

Just to be a good guy and a good friend, he waited until a few minutes before eleven before riding his bike over to Cody's. He was pretty sure Mrs. Hester was gone, but Hutch rang the doorbell just in case she was still there, knowing that wouldn't wake Cody, since Mrs. Hester liked to say doorbells weren't made to wake the dead.

When nobody answered, he walked around to the kitchen door, the one on the carport side of the house, knowing from experience it was always open if somebody was in the house, even if the somebody was still asleep.

Then he walked back to Cody's room, loudly opened the shades and yelled, "Rise and shine!"

From under his pillows Cody said in a muffled voice, "Aw, man, this is wrong."

"C'mon, dude, you can't sleep all day," Hutch said.

"But that was my plan," Cody said, wriggling himself deeper under his covers. "What time is it, anyway?"

"Eleven."

"*So* wrong," Cody said.

"We got to get out and play some ball."

"Not on our day off," Cody said.

He poked his head out from under the pillows and covers now, squinting.

"We're in the *finals*," Hutch said. "We got to get after it."

"Friday," Cody said. "Friday we're in the finals. Today is Monday. Please let me go back to sleep. I'll pay you."

"C'mon," Hutch said, pulling him up into a sitting position. "I won't even make you go all the way to Fallon Park, we'll just go over to the Community Center and play on the football field."

Fallon Park was about twenty blocks away. There were two baseball fields there, one for Little League and one for Babe Ruth, and a fenced-in batting cage with a ball machine that the coaches had keys for during the season. The fields weren't the best around, and there was always talk about tearing them up and building new ones if the city would ever come up with the money. But they were baseball fields. And because Cody's dad had once coached them in Little League, he still had a key to the batting cage.

"Nice of you," Cody said.

"Soooo nice," Hutch said. "I'm even going to buy you breakfast."

Cody got out of bed, as a form of surrender, mumbling, "I think I liked you better when you were suspended."

They stopped at the Kwik Stop, two blocks down from the corner of Gateway and Seacrest, for what Cody called

"the real breakfast of champions," which for him meant pow-
dered doughnuts and purple Gatorade. Then they rode their
bikes the rest of the way to the Community Center, went
around to the back, past the outdoor basketball courts that
were always patrolled, day or night. It was a good place for
kids of all ages, they knew, but the policemen you usually
saw there were a reminder to Hutch and Cody that their
Palm Beach County wasn't the one with mansions on the
beach.

Past the basketball courts and seldom-used tennis courts
was the football field used by the Boynton Beach Bulldogs,
who played in the South Florida Youth Football League. There
was a sign before you got to the field that read SUPER BOWL
CHAMPIONS, because a few years ago the Bulldogs had won
their big tournament, against the best teams in the country,
up in Jacksonville.

"Next week, I'm putting a sign like that on our front lawn
after we beat Orlando," Cody said.

"We're only playing for the state championship, Codes,"
Hutch said.

"From the best state in the country at producing athletes,"
Cody said.

"I thought that was California."

"Florida," Cody said, "and I have the stats to prove it."

"Where?"

"Right here," Cody said, pointing to his head.

They soft-tossed at first, then kept backing up, the way
Hutch would see guys doing at Marlins games when he was
lucky enough to go to Marlins games, until they were throw-

ing balls as far as they could. In this case, that meant from one twenty-yard line to another, even though Hutch knew he could have gone deeper than that if he'd wanted to.

There was no infield and no outfield and no bases. But they had green grass under their feet and a blue sky over their heads. The temperature was not only down in the seventies today, it felt as if somebody had thrown a switch and turned off the humidity.

The only thing that would have made the day better was having Game 1 be tonight. When they started throwing, even the smack of the ball hitting the pocket of his glove sounded better than ever.

"I think your arm got stronger in the last two days," Cody yelled.

Hutch yelled back, "Second basemen don't need an arm. I learned that watching you."

He uncorked his biggest throw yet, watched it sail over Cody's head.

"Sorry!" he yelled.

"No, you're not."

"You're right."

They had each brought a bat and hit fly balls to each other now, trying to outdo each other, even having a contest to see which one of them could be first to hit one through the goalposts.

Hutch won.

Cody said, "You hit it, you shag it."

Hutch said that was fine with him, he was just going to pretend he was running out a game-winning home run.

This was one of those days, he thought, when he could play baseball all the way until dinnertime.

It was when he reached down for the ball that he noticed the black town car in the distance, parked on North Seacrest.

Hutch didn't know if his dad was caddying today or driving, mostly because he hadn't done much talking to, or about, his dad the last couple of days.

Was that his dad's car?

Hutch knew there were always a couple of times a week when he drove mornings and then tried to caddy in the afternoon.

Was this one of them?

Another thing he didn't know about his dad.

But if it was his dad in that car, what was he doing *here*?

Why would he be watching him and Cody goofing around on a football field?

Hutch started walking toward the car, thinking if he got a little closer he might be able to see who was behind the wheel. Knowing he was probably being crazy, that there were probably more car-service cars like the one his dad drove around in than he could even imagine.

As he did, the car eased out behind a passing truck and pulled away.

• • •

His dad wasn't around for dinner that night. Hutch asked his mom if he'd been driving today and she said she actually wasn't sure, he'd been gone when she woke up.

"Why do you want to know?" Connie Hutchinson asked.

"Just wondering."

His mom said, "You never ask about your dad's work. Why tonight?"

Hutch pushed some food around on his plate. "I was just wondering why he wasn't here, is all."

"Are things any better between you two?"

"Same," Hutch said, not looking up.

"Well, that's not good," she said.

Hutch looked up at her now. "The other night Dad told me he'd been lying about his shoulder injury, that when he got to the minors he just wasn't good enough."

His mom had started to pick up her water glass. Now she put it down. "He told you that?"

Hutch nodded.

"That must have been very hard," she said.

"Me hearing that from Dad, you mean?"

"No," his mom said. "Him saying it."

"He could have told me before," Hutch said. "I don't know why he had to treat it like some kind of big family secret."

She said, "Maybe because only *he* knows what it was like going from what he'd been here to what he turned out to be *there*." She looked off and said, "And then ending up back here."

Usually Hutch helped her clear the table. Tonight she said she could handle it alone. So Hutch went upstairs to listen to the Marlins game, which is where he was when he heard the front door open and close.

He waited a whole half hour before he came down the stairs, hearing the television announcers broadcasting the same game against the Braves that Hutch had been listening to on the radio.

His dad was on the couch. If he had been driving earlier, he'd already changed out of his white shirt and tie and into a blue Florida Gators T-shirt and some khaki shorts.

The beer can was on the table next to him.

Hutch had planned to ask him whether he'd been at the Community Center, but somehow the sight of that beer, the force field being in place, made him change his mind.

Or lose his nerve.

And what did it matter, anyway?

His dad noticed him and said, "Hey."

"Hey."

It was about the normal length of the conversations they'd been having since Emerald Dunes.

Hutch stood there a little longer, knowing this night was going to be like all the rest, that he wasn't going to be invited to join him. Knowing at the same time he was never going to ask to join his dad, that if his dad wanted company he could just say so.

"'Night," Hutch finally said.

"'Night," his dad said, and took a sip of beer.

Hutch went back up the stairs, hearing the Marlins' announcers from his radio now, Dave Van Horne's voice rising as he described Hanley Ramírez trying to beat a throw home. Same game, same house, different broadcasts. Maybe it figured.

It was weird, Hutch thought to himself.

Two other shortstops in his life.

His dad was one, Darryl was the other.

And right before the biggest games of his life, he was barely on speaking terms with either one of them.

THE NIGHT BEFORE GAME 1, THEY GOT TO PRACTICE UNDER THE
lights at Roger Dean Stadium.

Hutch and Cody had both been there before to watch
spring training games, and once in a while would get a chance
to watch the Jupiter Hammerheads minor league team play
after spring training ended. So they knew their way around,
basically. Most of the time when they did get to come watch
games, especially ones involving the real Cardinals or the
Marlins, their favorite spot was this grassy area in foul territory down the right-field line known as The Berm.

It was underneath a picnic area known as the Party Deck
at Roger Dean, and tickets to watch from there cost only ten
dollars during spring training. When they did get a chance
to go, they'd always ask Mr. Hester to get them there in time
for batting practice—since they always went with Cody's dad,
never with Hutch's—so they could go straight out to The
Berm and compete with other kids for long foul balls.

And every time they were out there, Hutch and Cody
would tell each other how they were going to play on that
field someday, way before they ever knew you could do that
in American Legion ball when you were only fourteen.

Always when Hutch had imagined himself out here, playing for the real Cardinals or Marlins or even the Yankees, he imagined himself at shortstop. That's what he was, after all. A shortstop.

Tonight, and tomorrow night, and all weekend, he would be a second baseman. Hutch knew as soon as he stepped out of the dugout on the first-base side, got on the grass and stared out at the Budweiser scoreboard and the huge Bank of America video board in left center, that playing second base here would do just fine for now.

There was still plenty of daylight left when they took the field after Orlando finished their practice. But the lights were on anyway, just so players on both teams could get used to them, according to Mr. Cullen. Good thing, Hutch thought when he looked around. These lights weren't the ones they'd played under at Santaluces, as good as those were for town fields.

These were spotlight-bright. They were big-time. And somehow, playing on this field *under the lights* made everything feel even more big-time.

But then Hutch and Cody had been feeling pretty big about themselves from the moment they got out of the bus in front of the main entrance and walked across the little patch of green grass cut into the shape of a diamond, walked across that and between the two tall palm trees that felt like goalposts and underneath the huge white lettering that read ROGER DEAN STADIUM.

They had gone through their normal pregame drills, not changing their routine, and were finishing with batting practice now. Mr. Cullen had picked the order randomly tonight, Darryl going first and Hutch scheduled to go last. Cody had just hit and was standing on second base now, making his way around the bases every time Alex Reyes put a ball in play.

Hutch said, "It looks bigger from the inside, doesn't it?"

"Yeah," Cody said, "it does."

"Same dimensions as Santaluces, though," Hutch said. "Four hundred to dead center, 325 down the lines."

"I didn't notice," Cody said. "But you would."

Alex fouled one off, so Cody stayed where he was. "Maybe," he said to Hutch, "we should stretch this thing out to three games just so's we can *get* three games here."

"How about we just focus on winning Game One?" Hutch said.

"Okay, here we go with your 'one game at a time' crud," Cody said. "Blah blah blah."

Hutch grinned at his friend. "Funny," he said, "that's all I ever hear when you're talking. Blah blah blah."

Mr. Cullen was throwing BP, the way he normally did. Only tonight it didn't seem normal at all. Hutch could see that their coach was as happy and excited as any of them to be standing in the middle of this field tonight. Hutch watched him, listened to his constant chatter, saw the smile on his face, and wondered how many times in his life Mr. C had pictured himself under the lights on a big-league field, trying to throw fastballs past the world.

When it was finally time for Hutch to get his cuts, though, even Mr. C's best fastball wasn't fast enough. Hutch was on top of every pitch, hitting line drives to all parts of the field.

Hutch could see Mr. Cullen, who had been bringing it with everything he had, tiring. *Doesn't matter*, Hutch thought. *I'd hit him even if he was throwing 100. That's how well he was seeing the ball. This is what it must feel like to be Darryl every day.*

"No bunt," Mr. Cullen yelled in from the mound.

Hutch had taken the last of his cuts when Mr. Cullen yelled to him, "One more."

"How come?" Hutch said.

"Because I know I can get you out," Mr. C said, grinning.

Hutch shook his head. "Not today," he said. He didn't say it in a cocky way, or a trash-talky way, because he never looked to show anybody up. Especially his own coach.

But he was the last batter of the day and he could tell this was all for fun.

"Bring it then," Hutch said.

Mr. C said, "I'm warning you, I'm gonna dial it up now."

"Better dial 911 instead," Hutch said.

He cocked his bat. Mr. C threw him one last fastball. Hutch was sitting on this one the way he'd been sitting on the rest of them. As soon as he connected he heard that amazing sound he usually heard only from Darryl's bat, the one that was just different from everybody else's on their team.

Or in their league.

At first, Hutch thought this one might actually have the legs to get out of Roger Dean, especially when he saw Alex Reyes give up on it out in right center. But the ball finally landed on the warning track and one-hopped the wall over a Dunkin' Donuts sign.

And in that moment, Hutch was sure of something: He was going to hit a ball like this over the weekend, with a game on the line, or maybe even the whole series.

He didn't know why he was so sure.

But he was.

His dad wasn't there when he got home. His mom explained that a flight had been delayed coming into the West Palm Beach airport and his dad would have to sit and wait for the guy, some professional golfer, until he arrived.

But it didn't change the menu. In honor of the finals starting the next night, Connie Hutchinson said, she was making Hutch one of his favorite Puerto Rican dinners: *Asopao,* a thick gumbo that he loved, made with chicken, and *alcapurrias,* fritters, on the side.

She sat with him while he devoured all of it, asking him about Roger Dean, how practice had gone, wanting to know how excited everybody was.

A mom line of questioning if there ever was one.

During the school year she wanted to know everything that had happened to him during the day, every day. Hutch sometimes thought that she had just finally given up on getting his dad to talk about anything, and had decided to turn her full attention to Hutch and see if she could get him to open up.

But she never mailed it in, or acted as if she were going through the motions. She was genuinely interested in Hutch's answers, even when he thought he'd had a day that was duller than homework.

Tonight was different, though, and they both knew it. Hutch was pumped about having been on the field at Roger Dean and gave her a play-by-play of pretty much the whole practice.

"So we're ready then, is that what I'm hearing?" his mom said, smiling.

We.

Hearing *that* made Hutch smile. "Yeah, Mom, we're ready."

"Things okay with you and Darryl?"

One more time when she acted as if she'd heard a comment Hutch hadn't made, at least out loud.

"As good as they're going to be," he said.

"The old status quo," she said.

"If that means they are what they are, yeah, the old status quo," Hutch said. "Like with me and Dad."

"Honey," she said, "you and your dad are just going through a rough patch, is all."

Hutch thought: Yeah, a rough patch that started around fifth grade.

"Things will get better between the two of you," Connie Hutchinson said.

Hutch started to say something back, but just got up and took his plate over to the sink instead.

"What?" his mom said.

"I didn't say anything."

"Might as well have."

Hutch turned around. "Mom," he said, "you know how much I love you. But the only person who believes things are going to get better between Dad and me is *you*."

"Not true."

"*Totally* true, Mom, and you know it. He wants to act like we're alike, at least when it comes to baseball. But we're not. We're not anything alike, starting with how I'm not nearly as good as he was." He took a deep breath. "You want to know what else is totally true? We don't even have baseball in common, at least not anymore."

She didn't even try to bluff her way through with a smile. She just gave Hutch the same sad look she'd give his dad sometimes when she didn't think anybody was watching.

"Your father might not be able to express it, but he loves you very much and is very proud of you," she said. "And he'll be rooting for you as hard as I will this weekend."

"Right."

"He will, honey."

"He doesn't even want to be around me most of the time, even when he's here."

"Now you're being silly."

"No, I'm not. He'd probably be just as happy this weekend doing what he does best now: carrying somebody's bags."

"*You take that back, young man!*" Connie Hutchinson said.

Her voice seemed to explode out of nowhere in their tiny kitchen, the way a radio would when you turned it on and the volume was way too high.

Hutch didn't even know if she realized she had gotten up

from the table. But she had, her hands pressed down hard on the kitchen table, her face red.

"Mom—"

"Take it back."

Hutch knew he had no choice. He said in a small voice, "I take it back."

"Take it back like you mean it," she said. "Not because I'm angry at you, or because you want to get out of here. Take it back because it was a terrible thing to say and you ought to be ashamed of yourself."

Hutch said, "I'm sorry if it came out wrong. But that's what Dad does, isn't it? He carries guys' golf bags or he carries somebody's bags when he takes them to the airport, or picks them up, or whatever."

He was trying to calm things down, but he could see just by looking at his mom's eyes that she was still breathing hard, still on fire about this.

"You're acting as if this is the worst thing I ever said about anybody," Hutch said.

"Maybe it was."

"I don't get it."

"I can see that," she said. "So maybe it's time somebody explained to you how much strength it takes to be your dad. To carry *everything* around that he does."

● ● ●

They sat in Hutch's room.

No baseball on the radio now, the way there was almost

always baseball in this room at night. Just the sound of the fan and some night noises from outside and music coming from down the street somewhere.

Hutch's mom sat on the swivel chair at his desk, surrounded by all the shortstops on his walls.

"Mom," he said, "I didn't mean for this to turn into such a big deal."

"Well, it did, whether you meant for that to happen or not. And it *is* a big deal, whether you understand that or not."

"I wasn't trying to make fun of Dad, really I wasn't."

"No," she said, "you were doing something worse, and it wasn't just tonight. I've sensed it for a long time. The only *difference* tonight was that you finally put words to how you feel about your father."

"Feel what?"

He was sitting cross-legged on the middle of his bed, so he could feel the breeze from the fan.

"Ashamed," she said.

"No, I don't!"

"I'm not saying it's the only thing you feel about your father. I know you love him and it's more clear than ever to me how much you want his approval, and his support, when it comes to your baseball. But I know you are ashamed that he has to caddy for a living. And you're wrong to feel that way, as wrong as you've ever been about anything."

It was funny, Hutch thought, how quiet it seemed in here without baseball.

"He took me to Emerald Dunes," Hutch said.

He could tell it surprised her.

"When?" she said.

"The other night, after Darryl and I went at it."

"Nobody mentioned that to me."

"I thought it was just between Dad and me," Hutch said. "We hardly ever share anything. I figured it was okay to share a secret. If you could even call it that."

His mom turned around in the chair and looked out the window. "He took you there," she said, almost as if she were talking to herself now.

"Yeah," Hutch said, "and he told me that's where you end up if you care too much about baseball."

She turned back to Hutch. "He doesn't want *you* to end up there," she said.

"But it's okay for him?"

"Yes, it is."

"Why?"

"Because he's at peace there, that's why," she said, adding, "even though I'm not sure he understands that himself."

"Neither do I," Hutch said.

"What he's doing is good, honest work," she said. "He's with good players most of the time, and when he helps them play better, it's a way for him to compete. He takes pride in it. And he's outdoors, not stuck behind some desk in an office, which always drove him crazy."

"When you put it like that—"

"Let me finish," she said, holding up her hand. "He makes good money during the season, when the tourists are here, and does all right in the summers. When he puts that money with what he makes at the driving service, we do all right here. With a little help down the road, we'll have enough money to send you to college, whether you get the baseball scholarship your father thinks you're going to get or not."

"He never told me he thinks I'm good enough for a baseball scholarship."

"Because he doesn't want to put pressure on you," his mom said. "He wants you to keep playing for the love of it, not because it's a means to an end. He lost that love along the way, back when he became convinced that the only thing that mattered was making the big leagues."

This wasn't the night, Hutch knew, to say anything to her about the Hun School of Princeton, New Jersey.

Instead he sat there on his bed and wondered how come he and his dad seemed to communicate better when his dad wasn't even in the room.

Or in the house.

His mom stood up now.

"Cut him some slack," she said. "Your father's a proud man. If he thought working at that golf club was beneath him, he wouldn't do it. And he certainly wouldn't go back there at night the way he does when he wants to make peace with the way his life turned out."

His mother kissed Hutch on top of his head and left him sitting on the bed. When the door was shut, he immediately put on the Marlins game, lay there in the dark listening to it.

A half hour later, he heard his dad's car in the driveway.

Much later, about the seventh inning, Hutch went downstairs to get some ice water and saw that the television in the living room was still on, tuned to the Marlins station, and that his father's beer can was still on the table next to the couch.

But his dad wasn't there.

Hutch went outside, saw that his car wasn't there, either.

At least tonight, Hutch thought, *I know where he went.*

He was wrong.

GAME DAY.

At last.

Normally Hutch would have passed the time with Cody, trying to make the day go by faster, speeding everything up the way you did when you skipped through the boring parts of a movie on DVD. But today they could only hang together until just after lunch because this turned out to be the day Mrs. Hester had scheduled Cody to have his teeth cleaned.

"A trip to the dentist's right before the finals," Cody said as they were finishing their lunch at his house. "Dude, that is just plain dirty."

Dirty was one of Cody's favorite catchall words. If a pitcher threw a nasty pitch to get somebody out, the pitcher was dirty. Or the pitch was. And it was good or bad depending on whether the pitcher was yours or not. So basically there was good dirty and bad dirty.

In this case, having to go see the dentist on this particular afternoon was bad dirty all the way.

"I have a feeling you'll survive," Hutch said.

"What if he finds a cavity?" Cody said. "What if I need a

filling? There's a lot that could go wrong and then before you know it, he's reaching for the needle and the novocaine."

Hutch reached over, patting him on the back. "Look at it this way," he said. "I'm almost positive novocaine isn't on baseball's list of banned substances."

A half hour later, Cody left to go to the dentist. He told Hutch he could borrow his dad's key to the batting cage at Fallon Field if he wanted, but Hutch said no. He hadn't done that on the day of a game since the Cardinals' season had started and was superstitious enough, on game day especially, not to start doing that now; if he wanted extra hitting and the series did go three games, maybe he'd go over to Fallon on Sunday, an off day.

It was still only one in the afternoon. The game didn't start at Roger Dean until seven and the bus from Santaluces didn't leave until four-thirty. Hutch went to his room and turned on the fan and lay down on his bed and tried to think the happy thoughts his mom was always telling him to think, trying to visualize all the good things he wanted to happen against the Orlando Astros tonight. Connie Hutchinson was big on visualizing and even bigger on dreams, and chasing your dreams and achieving your dreams. For as long as Hutch could remember, she had been teaching him to visualize the way he wanted things to work out in his life.

Hutch lay there, alone in the house in the afternoon, closed his eyes, pictured line drives and diving plays in the field and runs crossing the plate for the Cardinals.

What he couldn't do was make the afternoon get out of

the way for tonight. Every time he'd look over at the clock on his desk, it was as if the hands had barely moved.

The way the clock in your classroom wouldn't move when you wanted a class to end.

His mom was at work. His dad, he knew, was at Emerald Dunes. There was no Marlins game for him to listen to on the radio or even watch on TV if he wanted. He thought about watching a movie on his computer, maybe the secondhand DVD of *The Natural* that he'd bought for himself at Blockbuster and nearly worn out by now. But he knew he wouldn't be able to concentrate, not even on the good parts. Not today.

So he came up with a better idea of something to watch, a dream that he didn't need to visualize because it would be right there on his own television:

His game-winning home run against the Yankees.

Yeah, Hutch thought.

I'll visualize the heck out of *that.*

It was when he came downstairs to get the cassette of the Channel 12 sports report that he saw the scrapbooks on the coffee table.

The ones of his dad's baseball career that his mom had lovingly put together.

Hutch couldn't imagine that his dad had taken them out to look at. So his mom must have had them out after everybody had gone to bed the night before.

The game stories out of the newspaper and the photographs had come from Grammy Hutchinson. Grammy hadn't been much at organization but she didn't like to throw anything out, either, and when they were going through her possessions after she'd died a couple of years ago, Hutch's mom had come across the big old box that had his dad's baseball career crammed into it.

Slowly, without telling anybody, Hutch's mom had gone to work on that box, finding stories from the *Post* that went all the way back to when his dad had played Little League. Finally she bought two beautiful leather albums, even though his dad had said they were way too expensive for a bunch of baseball games everybody had forgotten about.

"You haven't forgotten those games," she'd said to Hutch's dad. "And now neither will we."

His dad, seeing how important this was to her, instantly seeing how much work had gone into this gift, tried to act pleased then, sitting on the couch and going through the pages one by one, Hutch's mom on one side of him and Hutch on the other. But even that day, his dad sitting there with what had to have been the best years of his life right there in his lap, Hutch could see he was just going through the motions, acting the way he thought Connie Hutchinson wanted him to act.

If it hurt his mom's feelings, she didn't let on.

"I love them," he'd said when he got to the last page of the second book, the one that had a picture of him signing his first pro contract. "Thank you so much."

Then he did something he hardly ever did when Hutch was around. He kissed her.

It was the first and last time Hutch could remember him opening those books. Hutch hadn't opened them up again, either.

Until today.

He sat there in the silent front room in the quiet house in the middle of the day and looked at pictures of his dad in the Little League World Series in Williamsport, Pennsylvania, ones of him playing high school ball and holding up the state high school championship plaque, ones of his dad in his own American Legion uniform, so tight on him back in the day that it looked to be a couple of sizes too small.

There was his dad scoring the winning run when Post 226 beat Jacksonsville in the finals, when he was fourteen years old.

There was his dad, bat cocked, looking oh-so-serious, in the fake baseball card somebody had made up for him when he was a senior in high school.

Once Hutch opened the books up, it was as if he couldn't stop going through them. Maybe it was because his dad looked happy on the pages of these books, happier than Hutch ever saw him now.

He sat there on the couch and found himself wishing he could have known *that* Carl Hutchinson, the one who loved baseball this much once.

Too much, according to his dad.

Just once, Hutch wanted to see baseball make his dad look this happy again.

No, Hutch thought, not just baseball.

Me.

• • •

A woman from the American Legion Tournament Committee met them near the two palm trees outside Gate B a little after five, walked them through the stands behind the first-base dugout and around the picnic area before they finally came to the building behind the right-field wall where the real Cardinals dressed for spring training games.

Once they were inside the clubhouse, they saw the lockers for Albert Pujols and the rest of the team, saw where Tony La Russa's office was, felt the thick carpet under their feet.

Cody said, "I'm glad we're getting to play out *there*," pointing back in the general direction of the field. "But I'm pretty sure I want to live *here*."

Tommy O'Neill, who lived a couple of blocks away from Santaluces in Lantana, said, "This room is bigger than my whole house."

"Yeah," Chris Mahoney said, "but remember something: Tonight it's *our* house."

Most of the guys had gotten on the bus already dressed in their uniforms. Not Darryl. He had worn a T-shirt and cutoff jeans and sandals, and was quietly changing into his uniform now at Pujols' locker. There was, Hutch noticed, no wide-eyed wonder from Darryl about being in here, being on the inside, any more than there had been the night before when they'd first taken the big field for practice.

Darryl acted as if this was exactly where he was supposed to be.

Hutch thinking: Cody and me and the rest of the guys, we only dreamed about playing ball here someday.

Darryl *expected* to be here.

When Darryl had his spikes on and was good to go, Hutch walked over to him, put out his hand. Darryl looked up at him, waiting just long enough to make Hutch think he was going to ignore the gesture, just leave him hanging. But finally he reached up and casually gave Hutch a sideways slap.

"Let's do this," Hutch said.

He didn't expect them to suddenly be the best of friends just because they were in the finals. Tonight Hutch just wanted them to be the best teammates they could be.

Darryl just shrugged.

"I'm good," he said.

To the end, it was as if D-Will were a baseball team all by himself.

The guy's consistent, Hutch thought.

You've got to give him that.

• • •

Hutch saw a television cameraman near the third-base dugout when the Cardinals took the field, saw him aiming his camera and his TV light at two announcers in blazers, neither one of whom Hutch recognized. Sometimes the announcers would look at each other, sometimes straight into the camera, as if they couldn't make up their minds.

"What can they possibly be talking about?" Hutch said. "The game doesn't start for another hour and a half."

"Probably taping their standup," Cody said, as the Cardinals started to stretch in front of their dugout on the first-base side.

"Their *standup*?" Hutch said.

"I'm not just your average jock," Cody said in a smug way. "I know things."

They stretched and hit and took infield and now the minutes did start to fly by, until the Orlando players were being introduced first, lining up along the third-base line the way big leaguers did before Game 1 of the World Series. Hutch was watching from behind the screen in the Cardinals' dugout, taking it all in, noticing that by now a decent crowd had filled in the seats on the other side of the field.

Hutch knew it would be mostly friends and family for Orlando the way it would be for the Cardinals tonight, but he didn't care.

Inside his head, this baby was going to be standing room only.

When the public address announcer finally called out his name—"Batting third and playing second base for Post 226, Number Two, Keith . . . 'Hutch' . . . Hutchinson" —he jogged out to stand next to Mr. Cullen and Alex and Brett, slapped them all five, turned and saw his parents and Cody's parents behind the first-base dugout, in front of a whole row of blue Comcast signs.

Both Hutch's mom and Cody's started waving at him like mad when they saw him look in their direction.

Hutch, trying to be cool, just nodded.

Then he caught his dad's eye.

His dad nodded back.

He had made it in time.

He was here.

Like always, Hutch took what he could get.

Tripp was their starter for Game 1, against the Astros' ace, a seventeen-year-old right-hander named Rod Brown. There had been a story about him in that morning's *Post*, recalling the fact that he'd pitched a no-hitter in last year's final. The story also told how he had moved to Orlando from Austin, Texas, a couple of years before, and how his hero was Roger Clemens, another Texan.

He wore Clemens' number, 22, and was known to his teammates as "The Rocket."

The story said that the scouts in attendance tonight were primarily there to look at two players above all others:

The Rocket, and fourteen-year-old Darryl Williams.

"Nice write-up today," Hutch had said to Darryl during batting practice.

"'Bout time," Darryl said. "Wait till you see what they write at the end of tonight."

But through the first three innings, it was Rocket Rod Brown's night.

By the time he struck out Cody to end the top of the third—Orlando had won the coin flip before the game, making them home team tonight—it had been nine up and nine down for the Cardinals, with The Rocket striking out five guys already, including Hutch and Darryl.

The Rocket was everything they'd read about and heard about.

And more.

"So that's what a ninety-mile-per-hour fastball looks like," Cody said when he came back to the bench.

Brett said, "Don't you mean *sounds* like? I never saw the ball."

Fortunately Tripp was matching The Rocket out for out, if not strikeout for strikeout. So the game was 0–0 after three, the only hit so far coming from Orlando's leadoff man. Hutch and Darryl had vaporized him on the very next pitch from Tripp, on a 4-6-3 double play. Hutch flashed to his left to keep the ball from going into right-field and giving Orlando first and third, nobody out. He thought he might have to dive, realized he wouldn't have to, gloved the ball, spun around toward the outfield, and still managed to make a perfect throw to Darryl, who snapped off a Rocket-like throw of his own to get the runner at first by a step.

"That's what I like to see," Hutch said as he and Darryl ran off the field together.

Darryl nodded toward the people sitting in the seats behind the home-plate screen and said, "That's what the *scouts* like to see, homes."

Hutch doubled over first base with two outs in the fifth, not trying to pull the ball, just making solid contact. Darryl honed in with a runner in scoring position, doubled him home, and the Cardinals had the first run of the game.

Then Hank Harding singled home Darryl and it was 2–0. But Orlando came right back with two runs of their own in the bottom of the inning, Tripp getting wild and walking home one run and wild-pitching home another before getting a pop-up to end the inning.

When they got back to the dugout, Mr. Cullen informed Tripp that he was done for the night, explaining that if there was going to be a Game 3 Monday night, if the series did go the distance, he wanted Tripp to be as fresh as possible, even with two days of rest.

"One more inning, Coach," Tripp said. "Don't let me end my night with a sloppy inning like that."

They were at the end of the dugout closest to the water cooler. Mr. Cullen put his hands on both of Tripp's shoulders and said, "You know I was a pitcher myself once. So trust me when I tell you something, kiddo: Nothing has ruined more arms than guys thinking they had one more inning in them when they didn't. Okay?"

"Okay."

Mr. C said, "Now you go play first base and let Mahoney hold them until we get some runs and bring Pedro in to turn out the lights in the ninth."

The Rocket pitched one more inning than Tripp, through the top of the sixth, seeming not to tire, striking out the last three batters he faced: Cody, Alex, Tripp. All swinging. By Hutch's unofficial count that made it an even dozen strikeouts for the game.

All the Cardinal players, wanting this guy out of there as soon as possible, had noticed that Orlando had a new pitcher warming up even while The Rocket worked the sixth. But they weren't positive he was out of the game until they saw the new guy, a skinny right-hander, taking the mound for the top of the seventh.

"Look at him," Cody said. "I could use this guy to floss."

Hutch said, "You're assuming that they won all those games and got here with just one stud pitcher?"

"There's no way this new guy is as studly as the guy they just took out," Cody said.

"Don't be so sure," Hutch said, studying the new guy as he warmed up.

Then he got his bat and went and stood in the on-deck circle, because he was leading off the seventh.

Unfortunately, the closer Hutch got to the skinny kid, the better he looked. Even though he had an easy motion, pausing a little at the top, the ball just exploded out of his hand, the way the ball exploded off Darryl's bat even though he had that smooth swing. Hutch also noticed that the new guy had long fingers, always dangerous for a good pitcher, not just because they helped put more spin on the ball, but also because Hutch believed they could hold on to it a split second longer, generating more force and movement on it.

The public address announcer said his name was Julio Ortiz.

Julio threw two letter-high fastballs to start Hutch off, both of which he fouled off. The next two fastballs were just off the plate, Julio trying to get Hutch to strike himself out, Hutch being patient, not playing along.

Two-two.

Hutch tried to think along with the pitcher now, the way he always did, especially late in the game. He knew Julio didn't want to walk the leadoff man, not with Darryl waiting there on deck. And Julio probably didn't even want to go to a full count, put pressure on himself to *have* to throw a strike.

It meant that the next pitch might be the best one Hutch was going to see in this at-bat.

Had to be the fastball again. Julio hadn't thrown a single breaking ball yet and Hutch couldn't imagine him messing around with junk—if he had any—and risk hanging one now.

Hutch dug in, having processed all that in a few seconds, the way he could on a baseball field, in almost all situations, and dug in, thinking fastball all the way.

Julio threw him what looked like a fastball, what *should* have been another fastball, but what turned out to be the nastiest, dirtiest *split-fingered* fastball he had seen from any American Legion pitcher all season, which meant that it was the dirtiest splitter anybody had thrown him in his life.

The ball ended up in the dirt in front of the Orlando catcher, but it didn't matter because Hutch had swung right through the pitch. Forget about it, no chance.

As the Orlando catcher came out of his crouch to throw the ball down to his third baseman, Hutch said, "How much did that thing break?"

The kid lifted his mask, turned his head away from Hutch, grinned, and spat. "Enough," he said.

Hutch didn't just feel bad about striking out, he felt bad

about *looking* as bad as he knew he did striking out. And then he felt even worse about everything when Darryl—who'd obviously been paying close attention to old Julio from the on-deck circle—went the other way with the first splitter he saw, hitting a bullet into the right-field corner. When Hutch saw where the ball landed, he thought it would be a triple for sure. But Darryl, slowing down to check where the right fielder was with the ball, tripped over second base and nearly went down, and had to settle for a double.

Hutch thought: It would have been an *RBI* double if I hadn't been up there like I was swinging the wrong end of the bat.

Darryl made it to third when Hank Harding grounded out to second, but stayed there when Chris ended the inning by flying out to short left.

Game still tied, 2–2.

Stayed that way through the bottom of the seventh and through the top of the eighth. Before they took the field for the bottom of the eighth, Mr. Cullen had them collect at the home-plate end of the dugout, leaned against the screen to talk to all of them.

"Now we know we can play with these guys," he said. "All that's left is for us to *beat* them."

Chris Mahoney was still pitching. "I got this, Coach," he said.

Hutch said, "And we got you."

Then he said to everybody what he'd said to Darryl in the clubhouse:

"Let's do this."

When Hutch got out to second base, he looked around Roger Dean. He had been doing it all game long, just about every time there was any kind of break in the action. Checked out where his parents were still seated. Looked in behind home plate, trying to figure out which ones the scouts were. Not that *he'd* given them much to scout so far tonight, other than that one play in the first.

He turned around then, gave a quick look to the outfield, saw some younger kids out there on The Berm, watching this game from where Hutch and Cody had watched big leaguers play in the spring.

When he turned back around, watched Chris take his final warmup pitches, Hutch suddenly found himself hearing something Mr. Cullen would say on the bench during a close game:

"It hasn't happened yet."

He said it all the time in close games, and it always meant the same thing, that the play or the pitch or moment that would decide the game still hadn't happened.

In Hutch's mind now it just meant that the best of the night was yet to come.

Chris pitched a scoreless eighth for the Cardinals. Julio Ortiz did the same for Orlando in the top of the ninth. By then Pedro was warmed up and good to go, even in a tie game, ready to face the middle of the Orlando order. Usually Pedro was in there if they had the lead. Tonight he was supposed to keep the game tied and, somehow, get them to the top of the tenth.

On his way out to right field Cody veered off and came over to where Hutch was standing near the second base bag.

Cody said, "Do me a favor?"

"Sure."

"Do something great."

"Got it."

Pedro walked the No. 3 hitter to start the inning. It was not the way any of the Cardinals wanted to start the bottom of the ninth—putting the potential winning run on base.

Hutch didn't think the Astros would sacrifice with their cleanup guy, a lefty power hitter who played first, even if the guy on first—their center fielder—had great speed. But he was wrong. The sucker laid down a perfect bunt between Brett and Tripp, the ball rolling along the first-base line and nearly coming to a stop before Tripp grabbed it.

His only play was to turn and throw to Hutch covering first.

Winning run on second now, one out.

The No. 5 hitter hit the first pitch he saw from Pedro Mota down the right-field line, and when it came off his bat, Hutch was worried that it might be too far away from Cody for him to catch up with it. Cody could catch anything he could get to, but he wasn't fast and didn't get the greatest jump in the world, not even during batting practice.

Tonight he got a great jump, ran down the ball, and caught it in stride about five feet from the line.

Two outs now, but the runner on second had tagged and gone to third.

Hutch ran in to the mound, grinned at Pedro, and said, "You know our deal, right?"

"Get this guy to hit it to you?"

"There you go."

The Orlando catcher was built like a tree stump and Hutch knew by now that he had a short, dangerous, compact swing. He'd nearly driven one over Alex's head—not so easy to do—in the second.

But Pedro did as he was told, got the catcher to hit it to Hutch on a 1-2 pitch, throwing the kid a sinker of his own that was good enough—dirty enough—to have come spinning out of Julio's long fingers.

The best the kid could do was hit a high chopper toward Hutch at second.

Hutch knew the catcher had no speed, that he didn't have to charge the ball, that he could just wait on it.

The way the ball was bouncing, he didn't even need to use the old board move.

Until he did.

Until the ball hit the lip of the infield grass and went skidding across the dirt at a whole new speed, before Hutch had time to adjust and get his glove down in time.

The glove wasn't low enough and neither was he.

So he never even touched the ball as it rolled under his glove, through his legs, and toward Cody in right field as the No. 3 hitter for Orlando crossed home plate with the run that gave his team Game 1.

HUTCH DIDN'T MOVE AFTER THE GUY CROSSED THE PLATE.

He had made errors before; every kid his age made errors. Just never like this.

He had never lost a game all by himself like this.

They called it a walk-off home run when one swing ended a game in the bottom of the ninth. What did you call this—a walk-off E-4?

It was the biggest game he had ever played in his life, and it had ended on a nothing ball like that, going right through the wickets the way that ball had gone through Bill Buckner's legs in the World Series in 1986 against the Mets.

Now Hutch was Buckner, frozen in place between first and second at Roger Dean as the Orlando kids celebrated at home plate. He looked around at his teammates. Pedro Mota was finally walking off the mound, trying his best to avoid the celebration. Brett was already in the dugout, taking off his catcher's equipment so he wouldn't have to wear it on the long walk to the Cardinals' clubhouse out in right field.

Mr. Cullen just sat by himself at the end of the bench, staring out at home plate, watching the Orlando kids pound on each other like the series was already over.

Hutch didn't even want to look into the stands where his parents had been sitting with the Hesters, didn't even want to make eye contact with his dad.

Instead he just put his head down, staying right where he was, kneeling now in the soft infield dirt that was almost reddish in color, like a clay tennis court. That was where he was when he heard Cody's voice behind him, felt his friend's hand on his shoulder.

"C'mon," Cody said. "Let's bounce."

Hutch still didn't move.

"Codes," he said, "I make that play in my *sleep*."

"I saw the whole thing," Cody said. "I'm a second baseman, right? I saw how the ball stayed down on you."

"Now *we're* down a game, all because of me."

"Down but not out," Cody said. "So get up."

When Hutch still didn't move, Cody grabbed his arm and pulled him up and then the two of them were walking back toward right field together. Like always. Like they were walking something off. When they were nearly to the open gate in the outfield fence, a guy in a Sun Sports blazer who looked young enough to be one of their teammates got in front of them. He had a microphone in his hand and a cameraman with him.

All Hutch had been thinking about was how he'd let his team down. He'd forgotten, for the moment, that the game had actually been televised.

"Tim Fox," the guy in the blazer said to Hutch. "Sun Sports."

"I can see that," Hutch said.

"Ask you a couple of questions?"

Cody leaned in and whispered, "You're allowed to say no."

Hutch turned to Cody. "I let them talk to me on TV when I hit that home run."

"You don't have to do this," Cody said.

"Yeah, I do," Hutch said. "I'm captain of the team." He turned back to Tim Fox of Sun Sports and said, "Go ahead."

"How does it feel to lose Game One on a play like that?" Tim Fox said.

Hutch said, "I feel bad any time I make an error. I just feel worse tonight because I let my team down on such a bonehead play."

"What happened?" Tim Fox said. "When it came off the bat, it looked like you guys were headed for extra innings."

"I forgot the first thing my dad ever taught me in baseball," Hutch said. "To put my glove down."

Tim Fox thanked him and he and his cameraman ran toward the Orlando side of the field, done with the losers now. Hutch and Cody kept walking, past the thick yellow foul pole that had Metro PCS written on it, the letters running from top to bottom, through the gate, toward the clubhouse.

All season long Hutch had told himself he was still a shortstop, that nothing had changed, that he really wasn't a second baseman.

Well, tonight he'd proved it.

He *wasn't* a second baseman.

• • •

Mr. Cullen gave them a quick talk when they were back inside the clubhouse, reminding them of something he told them a lot, that the last play was never the only one that decided a game in sports, win or lose.

Even if a guy hit a grand slam in the last inning, he said, a lot of other things had to happen to get those bases loaded.

He wasn't talking to the team now and they all knew it. He was talking to Hutch, obviously under the impression that anything he said in here was going to make Hutch feel better.

As if anything anybody said was going to make him feel better between now and the start of Game 2, which felt about a hundred years away.

"I'm a Mets fan," Mr. Cullen said, grinning, trying as hard as he could to lighten the mood. "All you Yankee fans on our team know that. And Mets fans never forget Bill Buckner letting the ball roll through his legs in the '86 Series. But if you've ever seen the end of that game on one of those classics shows, you know how many other things had to go wrong for the Red Sox before Mookie Wilson dribbled that ball down the line."

Hutch wondered where he was going with this, thinking: *All I want to do is go home.*

"But before we go, I want to tell you about Game One of that Series, which only I remember," Mr. C said. "The Red Sox won that game. The score was 1–0. And you know how they got their run? On an error by the Mets second baseman, Tim Teufel."

Boy, Hutch thought, I feel so much better already.

"The Mets didn't let one play cost them their World Series, and we're not going to let one play cost us ours," Mr. Cullen said.

Then he told them to get their stuff together and start heading for the bus, it was time to call it a night.

Before long, Hutch and Cody were the only two players left in the clubhouse, in front of the last two lockers next to Tony La Russa's office.

The door opened and they saw Mr. C standing there, hands on hips.

"When I said 'start heading for the bus,'" he said, "what did you two hear me saying?"

Mr. C ran ahead of them, saying he was going to check the dugout one last time, make sure nobody had left anything. Hutch and Cody walked back through the gate in right, back across the outfield grass toward home. It was the same field it had been a few hours ago. Same dimensions: 400 to center, 325 down the lines.

It just looked different now.

When they got to the infield, Hutch said, "Maybe I should just dig myself a hole right here."

"*Awesome* idea," Cody said. "That way you could do what you want to do, and feel even lower than dirt."

"Codes," Hutch said, "you've played with me pretty much our whole lives, right?"

"Longer."

"You ever see me do anything like that in a big spot?"

"No."

"So why did I have to do it tonight of all nights?"

Cody stopped near the pitcher's mound. They were facing the dugout, where Mr. Cullen had come up with somebody's bat, and a batting helmet. They heard him saying, "Like picking up after my own kids."

In a quiet voice, so Mr. Cullen wouldn't hear, Cody said, "I'm gonna say this, and then we're not talking about this the rest of the night and I'm gonna make sure you stop feeling so sorry for yourself: It happened to you because it happens to everybody sooner or later, even if they've spent their whole career feeling like Captain Hero. Because we watched that World Series where the Tigers *pitchers* kept making errors on the simplest plays in the world. Because one of your Yankee heroes, Mo Rivera, probably the greatest closer in the history of the game, threw a simple ball away in Game Seven one time and the Yankees blew a whole World Series in the bottom of the ninth."

Mr. Cullen said, "Really, guys, we need for this night to be over now."

"Just one more sec, Coach," Cody said to him. To Hutch he said, "What do you always tell me when I ask *you* why some game ended in some weird way?"

In a voice even quieter than Cody's on the empty field, Hutch said, "I tell you that it's baseball."

"Baseball happened tonight," Cody said. "And I promise, baseball will be better tomorrow."

The bus was waiting for them near Gate B, everybody else on board by now, the engine running. Mr. Cullen got in ahead of them and took his usual seat in the first row. Darryl was alone in the seat behind him, slouched down, cap pulled down low. Good, Hutch thought. He didn't even want to make eye contact with Darryl right now, knowing that Darryl wouldn't even have to say a word to him, he could probably lay him out with one mean look.

Hutch thought about going all the way to the last row, sitting back there alone, even though he knew Cody wouldn't let him. But the last row was taken and so was the one in front of it, so Hutch grabbed the first empty window seat, on the ballpark side of the bus, took one last look at the lights of Roger Dean on this night, the night Mr. C said he wanted to be over now.

Not as much as I do, Hutch thought.

Cody sat down next to him, even though there were two empty seats across the aisle. In a voice just above a whisper he said, "I said all I'm going to say."

"Don't take this the wrong way, Codes," Hutch said. "But good."

"I'm just sayin'."

The bus pulled away from the Stadium, went past the Florida Atlantic sign, took a right on Donald Ross, then the left that put them on 95 South. There were guys talking, but they were all keeping their voices down. Usually there would be a lot of noise on the bus, even after they lost a game, the guys using jokes and laughter and insults to start putting the loss behind them.

Not tonight.

Hutch kept staring out his window. Even when the Cardinals *did* lose, there was something about the ride home, having the guys all around you, that made the game hurt less.

There was the feeling that it hadn't just happened to one of them, it had happened to all of them. And it was just another thing that Hutch loved about sports, being a part of a team, being a part of something, that people who'd never been on a team couldn't understand.

It just didn't feel that way tonight.

Tonight it was as if it had only happened to him, as if the rest of the guys had won and he'd lost, all by himself.

It was then that Cody Hester stood up.

"Okay," he said, "I've got a question."

Cody's voice was always loud. Tonight, because the bus was so quiet, quieter than it had ever been, his voice sounded much, *much* louder.

"It's about the end of tonight's contest," Cody said.

"Cody," Hutch said, his voice barely above a whisper. "Please don't."

Cody held up a hand to him. Like, not to worry.

"What do you think was worse?" Cody said. "Hutch's error, or . . . *Spider-Man 3*?"

"Spidey," Brett said. "No doubt. Too many bad guys."

"Okay, then," Cody said, "and moving right along." Sounding like one of those peppy game show hosts. "Hutch's error, or . . . that time we lost the Internet for a whole week because of the hurricane?"

"Not even close!" Hank yelled from the back. "No IM-ing for a whole week? It was like being in jail, dude."

Suddenly, everybody was calling out suggestions on stuff they thought was worse than Hutch's error. Hutch or the Marlins trading away all their good players the season after they'd won the World Series. Hutch or Season 6 of *24*, which prompted Cody to say, "Hey, watch it now."

Hutch's error or the creepy guy with the octopus face in the last two *Pirates* movies.

And now the bus was filled with noise, and would be all the way to Santaluces. Cody didn't sit back down, holding on to one of the overhead straps, until the ride was about to end and they were pulling into the school parking lot across from Field No. 1.

"See," he said to Hutch. "It wasn't the worst thing of all time. And if it does turn out to be the worst thing that ever happens to *you*, look on the bright side: It just means that the worst thing that is ever going to happen to you has already happened!"

"Codes," Hutch said, "you are truly certifiable. And the best friend anybody has ever had in the history of the known universe."

The bus doors opened and the Cardinals filtered out. Hutch and Cody stayed put, thinking they were the last two guys to leave. They weren't.

Darryl was still in his seat.

Cody made a motion with his hand, like asking him if he wanted to go ahead of him down the steps, but Darryl slowly shook his head.

Once Cody was gone, it was just Hutch and Darryl on the bus, the driver having gotten up to open the luggage hatch.

Great, Hutch thought, he's been waiting for me.

It wasn't enough that Hutch had been beating himself up since the game had ended. Now it was Darryl's turn to weigh in.

He still wasn't making any move to get up, was still lean-ing back against his window, his bare feet up on the seat next to him.

"Hey," he said.

"There's nothing you can say about the play I haven't been saying to myself," Hutch said. "I messed up big-time."

Darryl said, "Don't want to talk about the play. Ugly as it was."

"Thanks a lot," Hutch said.

"I just want to tell you one thing: We're still winnin' this. You got it?"

"Yeah," Hutch said.

"Don't say it 'less you mean it."

"Oh," Hutch said, "don't worry, I mean it."

For the first time, Darryl extended his hand first to Hutch, in the form of a fist. Hutch gave him some back.

"Let's do this," Darryl said.

He didn't wait for a reply, just got up, stretched like a cat, a very cool cat, and walked down the steps.

HUTCH WAS ON HIS BED IN HIS ROOM, LISTENING TO THE MARLINS-Dodgers game from Los Angeles, when he looked up and saw his dad standing in his doorway.

His dad never came up here at night when Hutch was listening to baseball on the radio. Hutch had never thought about it before, but it was as if this was his private place for Marlins games, the way the living room was for his dad.

Maybe without knowing it, Hutch had put up a force field of his own, just without the beer can.

"Hey," his dad said.

"Hey."

"Your mom asked me . . . " Carl Hutchinson began.

Even now, he had to be himself, not even act as if it had been his own idea to come up here.

"I get it, Dad."

"She thought you might want to talk, or whatever."

Tonight, Hutch thought. Tonight he wants to have another heart-to-heart talk. First he wants to do it when I get suspended, now when I feel even worse.

Yeah, Hutch thought, *good times.*

"Dad, I'm all talked out," he said. "But thanks for asking."

His dad stood there, as if waiting for Hutch to say something else. Or just tell him it was okay to go back downstairs and watch the game by himself, which was what Hutch was sure he really wanted to do.

"I played the game," his dad said in a soft voice.

Hutch sighed, the sound louder than he meant. "I know you played, Dad," he said. "Before the game, I was even looking through those scrapbooks Mom made for you. So I know you played, and I know how well you played, which is a lot better than I ever will."

It was as if his dad wasn't even listening, as if he were somewhere else. "I know what it's like," he said. "To lose."

Hutch sat up. "Not like this," he said.

He was suddenly very tired. Tired of talking about the game. Tired of even thinking about it.

"You'll get another chance tomorrow night to make up for it," his dad said.

There was a long pause from across the room and then his dad said, "Everybody deserves a second chance."

Yeah, Hutch thought, *they do.*

Just not tonight.

Then he rolled over on the bed, his back to his dad, and said good night.

• • •

Connie Hutchinson called Mr. Cullen in the morning and asked if she could take Hutch and Cody over to Roger Dean a little earlier than the bus was supposed to bring them, and he said it was fine with him, both the field and the clubhouse would be open by four.

Hutch and Cody didn't even bother going out to the clubhouse. They went straight to the field in T-shirts and shorts and spikes, hoping nobody else would be out there this early. And nobody was. But the infield had already been dragged, looked so new and clean Hutch almost felt bad about messing it up.

Of course, he'd done that the night before.

It was why he had work to do.

He went out to second and Cody went to home plate and started hitting him one ground ball after another, the ball against Cody's bat sounding even sweeter than normal because this was a big-league park and they had it all to themselves, the way they would when they'd get to Santaluces or Caloosa early for a game.

"We couldn't stay home and do this and take the bus along with everybody else?" Cody yelled out to him.

"If I'd known the field better," Hutch said, "maybe I would have been more careful on that ball."

Cody said, "Yeah, you're right, bad hops probably only happen here. I'm surprised that hasn't gotten out."

Hutch said, "Shut up and hit."

"Is that any way to talk to your best friend who's standing out here in the middle of a hot oven feeding you balls like he's one of those ball machines in tennis?"

"Sorry," Hutch said. "I meant to say: *Please* shut up and hit."

"That's better."

Hutch didn't miss one ball from the time they started

until he saw the rest of the guys filing in behind the first-base dugout and down the aisle to the field. None of the Cardinals even acted surprised to see him and Cody out there, having their own two-man infield.

The only person who said anything was Darryl, Darryl with his cap turned around backward even though he knew Mr. Cullen hated that, and wearing some new cool shades Hutch hadn't seen before.

"The two of you come here straight from breakfast?" Darryl said.

He didn't wait for an answer from either one of them, just walked casually toward the right-field fence.

• • •

Orlando got two runs in the first off Paul Garner.

Then they got two more in the second.

So it was 4–0 when Mr. C came out to talk to Paul, runners on second and third, still just one out. Hutch thought he might pull Paul, even if that would mean bringing in Tommy O'Neill, who hadn't pitched an inning since the semis of the county tournament.

But all their coach did was pat Paul on the butt and say something that got a smile out of him. Sometimes that was all he was out there for, to get a smile from a pitcher in trouble, and wouldn't leave the mound until he did.

Before he crossed back over the baseline, Mr. C brought the infield in, meaning they weren't going to trade an out for a run here. They would try to hold things at 4–0.

What they wanted here was a ground ball to Darryl or Hutch. But Hutch knew that was going to be easier said than done because Paul had been up with his pitches from the start.

Not now.

He finally put some late break on his first pitch to Orlando's No. 2 hitter, who put a good swing on the ball and blistered a one-hopper hard right at Hutch.

The ball was on Hutch so quickly he felt like a hockey goalie, dropping to his knees to make sure the ball didn't go through him because *nothing* was going through him tonight, gloving the ball cleanly, transferring it to his throwing hand in one clean move.

The kid on third, who'd taken off on contact, decided to test Hutch.

Maybe he just wanted to put more pressure on the second baseman who'd lost last night's game for his team. Or maybe he didn't know this particular second baseman had a shortstop's arm.

Whatever.

From his knees Hutch sidearmed a perfect throw to Brett, who had the plate completely blocked with his left leg. The kid coming from third had about as much of a chance of getting through Brett as he did beating Hutch's throw.

Yes! Hutch whispered to himself.

Two outs.

When Orlando's No. 3 hitter lined out to Alex in short center, the Cardinals were out of the inning, feeling much better than they had a right to, down four runs already.

"You wait and see," Mr. Cullen said when Hutch came down the dugout steps with the rest of the guys, all of them making a good baseball clatter on the wooden floor. "You just turned this sucker around."

"When we get some runs," Hutch said.

"You seem better today," Mr. C said.

"Having a game to play always makes me feel better," Hutch said.

The Orlando starter, a right-hander, wasn't a hard thrower like The Rocket, and had this herky-jerky delivery, snapping his head toward first base as he delivered the ball, not even looking at his target. He wasn't a submariner, his release point was higher than that. But he was definitely coming hard from the side, and first time up Hutch had trouble picking up the ball as it was released. He'd wound up lining weakly to second base.

He promised himself that he wasn't going to be late with his swing next time up. And he wasn't. With two outs, Cody on second, and Alex on first in the bottom of the third, Hutch worked the count full after taking five straight pitches. Hadn't taken the bat off his shoulder because he wasn't doing that until he felt like he got a good look at the ball.

He did so on the 3-2 pitch. It wasn't the best swing of his life, but he hung in there even though the guy dropped down a little more than he had and the ball seemed to come at Hutch out of the third base coach's box. Hung in and hooked one over the third baseman's head, the ball landing about two feet fair, rolling from there into the corner before the left fielder finally caught up with it.

Cody, off with the pitch, scored easily from second. No chance at him. But the Orlando shortstop thought he had a chance at Alex, which meant that he hadn't been paying much attention to the way Alex Reyes could run the last two nights. Alex beat the shortstop's relay in a breeze, sliding home just for the fun of it, Hutch taking third on the play.

Then Darryl lined one up the middle that nearly spun the pitcher's cap around on his head, and just like that the game was 4–3.

Now it really was what Mr. C had said:

Brand new ball game.

Paul pitched himself out of bases-loaded trouble in the fourth and kept the game at 4–3, then the bottom half of the Cardinals batting order started a small rally in their half of the inning, Cody finally doubling home Tripp and Tommy to give them a 5–4 lead.

Hutch looked out at Cody, clapping his hands at second base, the front of his uniform covered with dirt after his headfirst slide in there, and decided it was as fired up as he'd ever seen his friend on a ball field. Cody had gotten his biggest hit of the season, it had put them ahead, and best of all, he'd done it *here*. Here at Roger Dean, here in their World Series, here in a game they had to win.

Though neither Alex nor Brett could bring Cody home, the Cardinals had their first lead of the game despite starting out in that 4–0 hole. When Cody came off the field, Hutch was waiting for him with his cap and his glove.

"Now *that*," Hutch said, "that hit was *dirty*."

Cody grinned at Hutch, took his cap from him, took the glove, looked around Roger Dean as if he were seeing it for the first time, and said, "Dude, that was *mud*."

Orlando tied them in the sixth, the big hit coming off the

bat of Rocket Rod Brown, playing first base tonight. Paul left The Rocket stranded on third base but he was pitched out now, even though Hutch knew Mr. Cullen had wanted him to go a little deeper into the game.

The question now was who Mr. C would bring in to replace him. If they won tonight, there was going to be another game to play, and more relief pitchers to use, on Monday. But that didn't matter if they didn't win tonight.

He made his decision. When they were all in the dugout, Mr. C went over to Chris and said, "That rubber arm of yours got a couple more innings in it?"

Chris frowned like he was thinking it over, rubbed his shoulder with his left hand, and said, "I guess it feels fine, Coach. But you sure you want to waste me in a meaningless game like this?"

"I'll take that as a yes, wise guy."

"*Oh* yes!" Chris Mahoney said. "Tell Orlando to bring it on with their own bad selves."

Orlando made a pitching change of their own in the bottom of the sixth, bringing in a lefty. He was as tall as Rocket Brown but a whole lot wider, reminding Hutch of C. C. Sabathia, the double-wide who pitched for the Indians. The lefty showed you a lot of motion, so much that it was almost as if there was a little delay, like somebody had hit the pause button, right before he released the ball.

He was wild at first, walking both Hutch and Darryl to start the Cardinals' sixth, but then Hank bounced into a double play and Chris struck out and Game 2 was still tied.

Three innings left, unless they were still tied after nine.

It was different for Orlando, though, because they had that game in hand. The Cardinals *had* to win. Every pitch now, every hit or out in the game could *be* the game. Before the night was over, somebody was going to get the chance to make one of those swings—a scrapbook swing, Hutch thought— he'd remember for the rest of his life. Or maybe somebody would make the kind of error Hutch had made at the end of Game 1, remember *that* for as long as he played ball. Or even longer.

Hutch remembered Mr. Cullen's words to him the night he was suspended. "It hasn't happened yet." As he stood out near second waiting for Chris Mahoney to finish his warm up pitches, he thought: This is why you play.

It was everything. The stakes, the setting, playing to keep playing. All of that. But somehow it was even more than that. In a game like this, you knew what all your sports heroes knew. You had the same nerves, the same concentration, the same . . . *fierceness* to find a way to win the game. Somewhere tonight, Hutch knew, Jeter and the Yankees were playing a game, and even though it wasn't the playoffs for them, at least not yet, maybe it was a close game. Maybe the thing that was going to decide their game hadn't happened yet.

It made Hutch smile, knowing that wherever Jeter was, he couldn't possibly be into his game any more than Hutch was into this one at Roger Dean.

In that way, they were the same tonight.

Chris pitched a scoreless seventh. Orlando's double-wide used all his deception and off-speed stuff to go through

Tripp, Tommy and Cody after walking Paul to start the bottom of the seventh.

Two more innings to go. There was some kind of ending coming. Nobody knew what it was. Chris Mahoney breezed through the top of the Orlando order in the top of the eighth, looking as fresh as the first game of the season. If the Cardinals could just push across one lousy run, Mr. C could give the ball to Pedro Mota and he could pitch them to Monday night.

In the dugout, Darryl got up and walked all the way down from where he was sitting to where Hutch was sitting by himself near the bat rack.

"Gonna have to be you or me," Darryl said.

Hutch said, "We've got a lot of guys who can get us a knock when we need one." Not because he thought the other guys might be able to overhear, but because he meant it.

"Yeah, but it's not their *job*, homes," Darryl said. "It's *ours*."

Saying it matter-of-factly.

Like they were equals.

Darryl reached for where he'd left his batting helmet, on the top shelf of the bat rack. Hutch's helmet was so old and nicked up, it was as if a truck had run over it. Darryl's, even this close to the end of the season, looked as if somebody had just spit-shined it.

"It's on us," he said, "and everyone on this team knows it, whether they'd say it or not."

Hutch knew Darryl was right. Maybe you couldn't be as good as Darryl was without knowing it, without knowing who wanted to be up there in a big spot and who didn't. Even after last night, even after letting that ball go right through him, Hutch knew he wasn't afraid. He wanted to be up in this inning and when he got out on the field, he still wanted the ball coming to him.

Alex Reyes grounded out to second. But then their third baseman booted a routine grounder from Brett like he was a World Cup soccer player, booted it all the way into foul territory. And when the kid pouted for a second rather than starting to chase after it right away, Brett kept right on going after he rounded first and beat the throw to second with a sweet hook slide.

So they had the go-ahead run, maybe the winning run, on second with one out.

Ever since last night, everybody in Hutch's world had been telling him pretty much the same thing: Get them tomorrow. Well, here it was, this at-bat. Hutch figured he had waited long enough to square things. So he didn't wait past the first pitch he saw from the lefty. He jumped on a fat, hanging curve and hit it so hard to left that it was almost over the left fielder's head before he made a move on it. Brett could have walked home. It was 6–5, Hutch on second. Darryl singled him home on the first pitch *he* saw. 7–5. The inning ended that way.

Three outs from Monday night.

That close.

Except the game wasn't even close to being over.

• • •

Game in and game out, Pedro Mota was the most consistent guy on their team, the one who never seemed to get rattled, the one who clearly loved to be out there in close games.

He picked tonight to lose his fastball.

He wasn't throwing it as hard as he usually did, Hutch could see after a couple of pitches, and he couldn't locate it. And when both of those things happened to you at once, it didn't matter what league you were pitching in or what your numbers were, you were going to get rocked.

Pedro was getting rocked.

Orlando's first batter, their right fielder, doubled between Alex and Cody, to the Dunkin' Donuts sign in right center. The next guy drilled one right over first that looked like it might fall in the right-field corner for a double, but Tripp made an amazing play, diving to his left, not just getting his glove on the ball but holding on to it after hitting the ground hard.

Hard out, Hutch thought, in all ways.

Then, the Orlando center fielder, a switch-hitter, hit a hard grounder up the middle that neither Hutch nor Darryl had a chance at, and the guy from second scored easily. Just like that, still just one out, their lead was a single run, 7–6.

Hutch looked into the dugout at Mr. C, as if knowing his coach wanted him to look in there. Mr. C made a talking motion with his hand. Hutch called time and took his time walking to the mound to talk to Pedro.

"Don't try that Mr. C crap and try to get me to smile," Pedro said. "'Cause I ain't smiling."

"Take a look around," Hutch said. "No one is."

"I can't get the stupid ball to do what I want it to do," Pedro said, slamming down the rosin bag.

Hutch just stared at him, not saying anything.

"What?" Pedro said, as the home plate umpire took his mask off and came strolling toward them.

Hutch reached over, took the ball from Pedro, took his own glove off so he could rub it up hard, then slapped it back into the pocket of Pedro's glove.

"You're *not* giving up this lead," Hutch said. "And we're *not* losing this game. So suck it up and *start* making the ball do what you want it to."

Sometimes you had to take a different approach.

His little speech to their closer helped for exactly one batter, the left fielder, who hit a sinking liner to center that Alex made a sliding catch on for the second out.

One run ahead still, runner on first, one out away from Game 3, the little Orlando shortstop, littlest guy on their team, at the plate. Lefty hitter. A slap hitter, but one with a great eye who made you throw him strikes.

There was no chatter from the other infielders, just Hutch. "You got this guy, Petey," he called in to Pedro. It was Hutch's nickname for him. Pedro was Dominican and so was his hero, Pedro Martínez, and Hutch knew that some of Pedro's teammates used to call him "Little Petey."

The batter dug in, his bat raised, awaiting the pitch.

There was other noise all around him at Roger Dean, from both dugouts, from the stands, from the PA announcer who'd just announced the shortstop's name. But to Hutch, the field was quiet now, as quiet as his own room when there was no baseball on the radio.

He cheated a little bit toward second base, remembering that even when the shortstop had made good swings his first two times up, he had hit the ball the other way. But on a 2-1 fastball from Pedro that was right over the heart of the plate, one of those fastballs that just said "crush me," the little guy turned on the ball and pulled one to right.

At first Hutch thought the ball might hang up long enough for Cody to catch it, Cody charging hard toward the sinking ball. But it had too much topspin on it, finally knifing into the ground about ten yards ahead of him, then taking this crazy hop and spinning away from Cody, toward the line.

With two outs the kid from first was running all the way as Cody chased down the ball. Hutch was running, too, because it was all happening at once now at Roger Dean, the way it could in baseball, the runner running around the bases and the fielders going to their spots.

Hutch glanced over his shoulder, saw the Orlando third-base coach windmilling his right arm, waving the runner home, then looked toward the outfield and saw that Cody was already up with the ball and throwing home.

Hutch couldn't remember a time all season when Cody had thrown out a runner at the plate, but he had to do that now or the game was tied.

Tripp was set up perfectly as the cutoff man, really only there to give Cody a target because there was going to be no cut. It was do or die now. That kind of play.

Cody's throw had a little too much air underneath it but had plenty of juice, too. The problem was it was on the wrong side of the first-base line, heading over Tripp's head, sailing into foul territory instead of toward Brett at home plate.

But Hutch was there.

He had come running from second base to be right there, be where Jeter was that night against Oakland in the play-offs, was running for Cody's throw the way a wide receiver ran after a pass in football.

He didn't pick the ball up off the ground the way Jeter did against the A's that night. Hutch caught this one in the air, all of his momentum going toward the Cardinals dugout behind first base.

Even running away from the plate as he was, Hutch turned his body midair and flipped the ball to Brett, who had the plate blocked like a champion. Brett: who caught Hutch's throw a split second before the runner came pile-driving into him.

Hutch was on his knees again as the game ended, the way he had been the night before. He was on his knees a few yards inside the baseline, about halfway between home and first, holding his breath, watching Brett until he came rolling out from underneath the Orlando runner and showed the umpire his catcher's mitt.

And the ball was still inside it.

Then the silence was over and this is what Hutch heard: "Out!"

Then before Hutch could move, the ump was running

over to him, reaching out a big hand to help Hutch to his feet, shaking Hutch's hand as he did.

"Thanks, kid," the ump said.

"For what?"

"For showing me somebody could make that play *twice* in my life. I'll see you Monday night."

Hutch didn't watch himself on the eleven o'clock news when he got home.

He hadn't watched when he'd lost Game 1, and he wasn't going to watch when he saved Game 2, either. The ending was better this time, but it was the same deal as Friday night: No matter how many times he watched himself, the final score wasn't going to change.

And the only reason he knew that the *Post* had called him "Jeter Junior" in Saturday's paper was because Cody called and told him all about it, not even waiting until Mrs. Hutchinson drove them to practice.

"You really didn't look at the paper this morning?" Cody said in the car. "Scout's honor?"

"*Scout's honor?*" Hutch said. "Cody, you went to exactly one meeting before you quit Boy Scouts. And, no, I didn't look at the paper, ask my mom."

Connie Hutchinson said, "He didn't even check the box scores today, which usually makes me take his temperature."

"All I can say is, they liked you a lot better today," Cody said.

"So do I," Hutch said.

Mr. Cullen had said he wanted a short practice today, just so they wouldn't have nearly two full days to think about Game 3. No heavy lifting, he promised. Just some BP and a little infield. Tripp could do a little light throwing on the side if he wanted to, along with Pedro and Chris Mahoney. One hour to be together as a team before he gave them the rest of Sunday off.

When they finished a few minutes before two, they all sat down under the green canvas roof over the five rows of bleachers at Field No. 1 and swigged Gatorades and water as Mr. Cullen faced them.

"They had their chance to knock us out last night and they couldn't do it," he said. "That's why this thing is ours now. They know it and we know it. Am I right?"

They all nodded.

"Their time is over," he said. "It's done. This is our time."

Cody raised his hand.

"Uh, Coach?" he said. "Isn't that exactly what the coach said in *Miracle* right before the big Olympic hockey game against the Russians?"

"Kurt Russell," Brett said.

"No, the coach was Herb Brooks," Hank said.

Brett said, "I *know* who the coach was. I mean the actor playing him."

Mr. Cullen grinned. "You got me," he said to Cody. "I just didn't know if I'd ever have a chance to give that speech."

Everybody had a good laugh at their coach's expense. Then their parents began to show up, and the long wait until Game 3 had officially begun.

• • •

Early Sunday night.

Cody had gone home after eating dinner with Hutch and his mom, Hutch's dad having had to make another one of his unexpected airport runs.

Hutch's plan was to watch *Sunday Night Baseball* on ESPN, at least until his dad came home and reclaimed the living room and the couch. The Yankees were playing the Red Sox, which meant Hutch would get a chance to watch the real Jeter in action.

Except he wanted to be in action himself.

He knew he was only kidding himself if he thought he could hang around the house and relax and not think about playing Orlando in less than twenty-four hours. He needed to get outside, move around, even with Jeter on television, do some baseball things.

He called Cody and asked if they could use his dad's key to the batting cage at Fallon Park, go hit some balls.

"I have played enough baseball this weekend," Cody said. "And so have you. You can take one night off."

"I know I *can*," Hutch said. "I just don't *want* to. Is it all right if I borrow the key?"

Cody said that he was acting like a crazy person but, yes, he could borrow the key.

When Hutch told his mom where he was going, he could tell by the look on her face that she thought he was acting a little crazy, too. But she said he could go ahead.

"For one hour," she said. "And if the park is empty, you

promise you will turn your bike around and come straight home?"

Hutch said he would, even though he was sure there was some kind of men's softball league that used Fallon Park on Sunday nights.

He didn't even bring his glove with him, just his bat, slinging his bat bag over his shoulder for the bike ride. He ran into the Hesters' house, grabbed the key from Cody, who told him he was crazy again, then rode the twenty blocks to Fallon, for his own early batting practice, twenty-four hours before the game.

There was a softball game going on under the lights, just as Hutch suspected. Usually he would stop to watch any kind of ball game, but he only had an hour, so tonight he rode right past the big field at Fallon, past a couple of tennis courts, out toward the secluded spot behind the Little League field where the lighted batting cage was nearly hidden by a cluster of palm trees.

Before he got there, Hutch could hear the crack of the bat.

Not an aluminum bat.

A wooden bat, making the sweetest baseball sound in this world.

Except it wasn't a sweet sound tonight. It was the opposite of that to Hutch, because it meant somebody else with his own key had beaten him to the cage, on tonight of all nights.

Hutch got off his bike, leaned it against one of the palm trees, and poked his head around it, curious to see who else wanted to come work on his swing on a Sunday night.

When he did see, he couldn't believe his eyes.

The guy in the cage was his dad.

• • •

Hutch stayed behind the palm tree, not wanting his dad to know he was watching him.

He still couldn't believe his eyes, that it really was his dad, taking his stance and waiting for the wheel with the balls in their separate holders to turn slightly toward him, then coming forward with his bat when the pitch was delivered, his swing looking as smooth and level as Darryl's.

Hutch didn't even know that his dad still played baseball, or that he had a key to this batting cage, because he had never mentioned the key to Hutch or offered to let him use it, even when Hutch and Cody would talk about coming over to Fallon to hit.

But here he was, as serious standing in there waiting for the next pitch as if he were the one getting ready to play the title game. As serious as if he were standing in there against a real fastball, or curve. He wasn't wearing a helmet, which the sign outside the Fallon cage told you to do if you were going to use the ball machine. He just wore an old Braves cap Hutch had never seen on him before, the A in white script, a dark blue cap with a red bill. His dad wore that and a gray sweatshirt with the sleeves cut off up to his shoulders, showing off the ripped muscles in his upper arms.

No batting gloves. Like me, Hutch thought. Bat held high. No flipping motions with the bat like you saw from some big leaguers, the ones waving the bat behind them as they waited for the pitcher to pitch. While Carl Hutchinson waited for the next pitch to come to him, he was almost completely still. Hutch had a clear view of his dad's face. Under the lights in the hitting cage, Hutch could see his dad's eyes focused on the ball as if it were the only thing in the world that mattered right now.

Then another ball was on top of him and he was coming through with his arms and wrists and hands, the wood bat so loud on the ball Hutch was sure they had to be able to hear it back at the softball game, this hit rocketing right off the ball machine itself, so hard that Hutch thought it might knock the sucker right down.

Hutch shook his head, thinking: He *smoked* that one.

And in the batting cage, Hutch saw his dad smile then, smiling the way he did in the scrapbook pictures. Smiling as if he were young again.

In that half-light you get between day and night, darkness coming faster now, Hutch heard his dad say *"Yeah"* to himself. Then his dad took his stance again, and as the ball was coming to him, he dropped his bat down and got it out in front of him and laid down what looked to Hutch to be a perfect bunt. The way you would if you were having real batting practice.

The ball he bunted must have been the last one, because now he walked up to the machine and began picking up all the balls around it, the ones he had rocketed into the netting and sometimes through the netting and into the wire fence around the cage at Fallon.

Hutch could hear his own voice inside his head, loud now, so loud he was almost afraid his dad would be able to hear it, telling him to get out of here before he was spotted. And maybe it was something else telling Hutch to leave, maybe the idea that this was his dad's own little baseball world and somehow that Hutch was intruding on it. That Hutch should just leave him here in this cage with his memories.

Hutch stayed where he was.

He didn't know what he would tell his mom when he got home, didn't even know if his *mom* knew that his dad still came to batting cages. Hutch hated to lie about anything and hated even the thought of lying to his mom more, but he could hear himself telling her that he'd changed his mind about Fallon, that he'd just decided to ride his bike around for an hour and start imagining all the good things that were going to happen to him in Game 3.

Maybe there'd be enough truth in what he'd tell her that it wouldn't really qualify as a lie.

Or maybe this was something he could talk to his mom about, even if he had to swear her to secrecy about spying on his dad this way. Maybe she knew that this was another place his dad went to find peace, even if he was doing it in a batting cage, even if he was using *baseball* to find peace when it was baseball that was supposed to have made him so torn up in the first place. And so sad.

He remembered the other night when he had come downstairs and found the TV set on and the beer can on the end table, and he'd just assumed his dad had gone over to Emerald Dunes to walk around. But maybe Hutch had been wrong, maybe watching the game had made him want to grab a bat and come here.

One by one now his dad placed the balls back into the pitching wheel, taking his time, as if he were enjoying even this part of the process. When he had the machine loaded up, he jogged back to pick up his bat and get back into his stance, as if he didn't want to miss a single pitch.

"Bring it," he heard his dad say to the ball machine.

Then *he* was bringing it again, never overswinging, never looking as if he were trying to jack one right through the chain-link fence and out of the cage. He just stayed back, patient, the way the best hitters were, his weight back to start before he cleared his hips, sometimes keeping his head on the ball so long, or at least where the ball had been before he smacked it, that it looked to Hutch as if his head were still down when the ball was into the net.

Hutch kept picturing the balls rolling all the way to an imaginary wall for extra bases.

Every few seconds at Fallon Park there was the crack of his dad's bat on the ball and that was the only sound at Fallon except for an occasional burst of laughter from the softball game in the distance. Hutch remained hidden behind the tree, just his head poking out, as he watched the boy in his dad come out with every swing.

Finally they were sharing baseball, even if only one of them knew it.

Everybody had left the Cardinals' clubhouse and gone out to start stretching before Game 3.

Everybody except Hutch and Darryl.

It was nothing new for Darryl. He was always the last one on the field for stretching, sometimes not even stretching at all, as if he couldn't be bothered.

But tonight Hutch was with him, taking his time putting some black electrical tape he'd found in the trainer's room around the toe of his right baseball shoe, having looked down as he was getting dressed and noticed that the whole front of the shoe had come loose from the sole and was just sort of flapping around.

Hutch had thought he could make it through the whole season with these shoes, a pair of mid-length black Nikes, but now he'd come up one game short. So he sat in front of the locker he was using tonight and took his time being a shoemaker. The locker had David Eckstein's name over it. He was the Cardinals shortstop, the little guy with the dirty uniform and a ton of heart who'd been the MVP when the Cardinals won the World Series a couple of years ago. Another baseball team that wasn't supposed to win, and somehow did.

Usually Hutch would be rushing to finish the job, rushing to get on the field with the other guys. But for some reason he was enjoying the last of the waiting time tonight. He couldn't have explained it to anybody if he tried, but after being impatient all afternoon, counting down the minutes until it was time to go over to Santaluces and get on the bus, he was fine now with the last quiet he was going to get before he got outside.

So he was in front of Eckstein's locker and Darryl was across the room in front of Pujols'. Hutch couldn't remember a time all season when it had been the two of them alone, really alone, like this.

Right before he finished up with the last piece of tape he'd ripped off, Darryl came across the room and sat at the locker next to him, the one belonging to Adam Wainwright, the Cardinals' young starting pitcher who'd been the closer on the Series-winning team.

"Tell you what," Darryl said. "We win tonight and I'll give you a brand-new pair of shoes." He nodded at Hutch. "What size are you?"

"Nine."

"Same as me."

Hutch said, "You always seem to have new shoes. Like you get a new pair every time you get a new pair of shades. How does that work?"

Darryl shrugged. "People give me stuff. Maybe thinkin' that when I make it to the big leagues and the big money starts rollin' on in, I'll remember they were nice to me back in the day."

Hutch grinned. "*When* you make the big leagues? Not *if*?"

Darryl shrugged again. "No worries," he said. "No doubts."

Hutch thought: Not only are we talking to each other like teammates are supposed to, Darryl's the one who started it.

Maybe it was because it was their last night as teammates, maybe it wasn't any more complicated than that.

"That ought to do it," Hutch said, making sure the last piece of tape wasn't covering one of his spikes.

"Both your folks gonna be here tonight?" Darryl said.

"Yeah," Hutch said, "though I sort of always have the feeling that my dad would just as soon be somewhere else. Anywhere else, actually."

"Man," Darryl said, his voice rising suddenly, like he'd gotten disgusted with Hutch all over again, "you talk some stupid dang smack for a smart guy sometimes."

Hutch looked up from the floor to see if he was kidding, even though Darryl Williams had never been much of a kidder, not that Hutch had ever noticed. But he could see from Darryl's face that his mood had changed.

That he was back to being the old Darryl.

"What kind of smack?" Hutch said.

"'Bout your old man."

"All I said was—"

"I heard what you *said,* homes," Darryl said. "Heard what you said and see the way you act toward your old man, way you talk about him sometimes when you think only your boy Cody can hear. Boo-hoo, my daddy don't care."

"Hey, take it easy," Hutch said. "You don't know what you're talking about."

"Yeah, homes, as a matter of fact I *do*."

"Guess what," Hutch said, not wanting to get into this now, but not being able to help himself. "Not even I know my dad." Thinking back to last night now, the batting cage at Fallon Park, thinking that last night might have been the closest he ever came to knowing his dad without a word between them being spoken. "So how come you know both of us so well all of a sudden?" Hutch said. "'Cause he worked you out one time?"

Hutch looked up at the clock. He had been taking his time taping his shoes. But now he did want to be on the field, didn't want to waste any more time with this. Whatever this was.

"Want to know what *I* know about your old man?" Darryl said. "That he's *here*. Seriously. When you look up over our dugout tonight, where's he gonna be?"

Hutch said, "That's not what I meant—"

Darryl waved him off. "He's gonna be there, that's where he's gonna be. Watchin' you play." Darryl shook his head. "My mom's comin' tonight, too. For the second time all season, I figure. You know why only twice? 'Cause she's too tired when she gets home from bein' on her feet all day. Tell me somethin' here, Captain: You think your old man *ain't* too tired to come watch baseball after carryin' some rich man's golf bags all day?"

It was coming out of him now, like this was something he had saved up all season.

About somebody else's dad.

Darryl said, "And by the way? You know the next time I figure my old man's gonna show up for one of my games, if he's even still alive? When I'm at Yankee Stadium someday, or some such. That's when he'll probably want to start up with all his father-son stuff. When there's something in it for him other than me."

Hutch stood up. "D, this isn't the place for this, we gotta bounce here."

Darryl was still sitting in his chair, acting as if he had all night.

"I know where we gotta go and where we gotta be," he said. "I just had to tell you because I didn't know if I'd ever get the chance after this game here tonight: You oughta stop actin' like such a baby on account of what you *don't* got. And be a lot happier, and more grateful, for what you *do*."

He stood up.

But he wasn't through.

D-Will said, "Be happy that when you are looking up in those stands tonight, you're gonna see what I never saw one day of my life."

He walked through the door. Hutch followed. Late in the season, real late, he was finding out he didn't know nearly as much about the two shortstops in his life as he'd thought he did.

THERE WERE NO INTRODUCTIONS ON THE FIELD TONIGHT THE WAY there had been before Game 1.

They did bring out representatives from Post 38 in Orlando and from 226, and there was a young woman in an Army uniform who stood near home plate and sang the National Anthem better than Hutch had ever heard it sung before.

So there was *some* ceremony tonight, even if it didn't take nearly as long as it had on Friday night, which already seemed like a long time ago to Hutch. It was as if all the big shots from the American Legion wanted to make sure everybody at Roger Dean realized this was still a special occasion.

As if anybody playing in the game needed to be reminded, Hutch thought.

He didn't need songs or flags and he was sure nobody else on the team did, either.

Mr. Cullen won tonight's coin flip, making the Cardinals the home team, meaning they had last ups again, just like they wanted. When he came back into the dugout, he called them all together in front of their bench.

"I'm gonna keep this short, and simple," he said in a voice so quiet, Hutch wondered if everybody could hear. "Boys, if you're lucky, you might get a handful of games like this in your lives. I don't know how many, nobody does, that's why you play. But what I *do* know is this: You've all got one tonight." His voice got a little bigger now. "And what I guess I want to ask you is if you came here to lose the sucker."

"No!" they yelled, loud enough for the whole ballpark to hear.

"Are you still too young?"

"No!"

"*Is* this your time?"

"Yes!"

He put his hand out. They all reached in. "Now go make this a night nobody can ever take away from you."

They broke their huddle and ran out from behind the dugout screen and took the big field.

• • •

Rocket Rod Brown was throwing even harder tonight than he had in Game 1, even with just two days' rest. Nine up and nine down through three innings, six strikeouts, only one ball—a fly ball to left by Darryl in the bottom of the second —out of the infield.

"This is beyond dirty," Cody said after striking out looking to end their third.

"Long way to go," Hutch said.

"I'm aware of that," Cody said, taking his glove and cap

from Hutch. "But that last splitter he threw me? That was pure filth. If it's a movie, it's got one of those ratings where nobody under seventeen is allowed to go."

"We'll get to him," Hutch said.

"When?" Cody said.

They were already trailing 2–0, because of a two-run Rocket home run. And while Hutch was never going to admit this, he was starting to wonder just when they were going to do anything against Orlando as long as the Rocket was still pitching the way he was.

When they finished throwing the ball around before the start of the fourth, Hutch ran in for a quick chat with Tripp, who'd really only thrown one bad pitch so far—the one Rocket had hit over the 325 sign in left.

"One thing?" Hutch said, taking the ball from Tripp and rubbing it up for him.

Tripp said, "What?"

"No more runs."

Tripp got through the top of the fourth, one of the outs coming when Hutch ran like an outfielder toward short right and made an over-the-head catch on a ball the Orlando shortstop had hit. Then the Cardinals came to bat in their half of the inning.

It started innocently enough, with a walk to Hutch. But Hutch then stole second on the first pitch to Darryl, the first time all game the Cardinals had a runner in scoring position. And with the Cards' best hitter at the plate in the form of Darryl, the Astros must have figured Hutch would stay put and let the hitter do his job. Maybe that's why the Rocket didn't even look back at Hutch when he had Darryl 0-2 in the count.

Hutch kept walking into a bigger lead. And as soon as Rocket went into his motion, he took off for third.

Didn't even draw a throw.

The pitch was high and Darryl laid off it for a ball.

The extra stolen base seemed to knock Rocket off the rails for a second. He overthrew his next pitch—a splitter that bounced about two feet in front of the plate and away from the Orlando catcher toward the Cardinals dugout.

Hutch didn't hesitate, he was coming home all the way. Their catcher got to the ball fast, and the Rocket was off the mound to cover the plate almost as fast. But Hutch beat the play with a straight-on slide and the score was 2–1 now.

"Cheap run," Rocket said when they were both still down on the ground, even giving Hutch a little shove as he stood up first. "Cheap, cheesy run."

Hutch bounced up now, ignoring the shove, since the last thing he was going to do was get into it with their pitcher in a game like this. He did point out at the Bank of America scoreboard, though. "Check it out," Hutch said. "They're gonna put the run on the board anyway."

Darryl flied out to deep center to end the inning. Yet at least the Cardinals *were* on that scoreboard now. They were still getting no-hit. But they weren't getting shut out. It felt like something, maybe even more than just one run. It felt like hope, even the way the Rocket was still bringing it.

It stayed 2–1 through the top of the fifth, even if it was a struggle for Tripp. He managed to get through the first four guys in the Orlando order without giving up another run, but needed thirty pitches to do it, the third out coming on a vicious line drive from Rocket Brown into Hank's glove at third.

In the dugout, Mr. C told Tripp that had been his last pitch of the night.

"Please let me stay in," Tripp pleaded when he got to the dugout. "I can hang in there against this guy, I know I can. I can stay out there as long as he can."

"Son," Mr. C said, "you've already done the thing that makes everybody want to play this game in the first place."

"What's that?"

"Been even better than you thought you could be," Mr. C said, and then shook his hand and told him to go get his first baseman's mitt.

The Cardinals went quietly in the bottom of the fifth, and there was a slight delay when Chris Mahoney came out to pitch the top of the sixth because Rocket's landing spot had created a huge divot at the bottom of the mound, one the groundskeeper needed to fix.

It gave Hutch a chance to take another look around.

Like taking one more snapshot of the night.

His parents were in the same seats they'd been in for the first two games, the last row in front of one of the Comcast signs. Mr. and Mrs. Hester were next to them. And next to Mrs. Hester was a woman Hutch had never seen before, but who looked too much like Darryl *not* to be his mom.

Hutch couldn't help but smile.

• • •

The Orlando right fielder singled with one out in the top of the sixth. When Cody fumbled the ball in right center, the kid kept going and made second standing up. Their second baseman was next up and bunted the first pitch toward third, attempting to sacrifice with one out. Maybe the thinking in the Orlando dugout was that if they could get the guy over there, they could get one of those cheap, cheesy runs Hutch had gotten.

Hank picked up the ball with plenty of time to throw the runner out at first, but for some reason he rushed, maybe the nerves of the moment grabbing him by his throwing arm. The ball bounced in front of Tripp at first and when he couldn't come up with it cleanly, everybody was safe.

First and third, still just the one out, the Orlando left fielder coming up. Mr. C waved the infield in, not wanting to give up another run here even if it meant giving up a shot at a double play. Because if they tried for a double play on some kind of slow roller and didn't get it, the game was going to be 3–1. A lead like that, the way Rocket was pitching, was going to feel like a lot more than two runs. And Hutch was starting to worry that the guy might have it in his head to go the distance.

So if the ball was hit to Darryl or Hutch, they were coming home if the runner from third tried to score. Or they were going to hold him there and get an out at first. That was the plan, anyway.

Before Chris went back to the mound, Darryl called over to Hutch.

"Hey."

Hutch shot him a quick look.

Darryl said, "It comes to us, we got this, right?"

And somehow Hutch knew exactly what he meant without asking. Just knew. Somehow, in the last game, they were finally on the same wavelength. They were never going to be friends. They might not ever play together after tonight.

They were just two teammates trying to figure out a way to win the game.

At 2-2, the left fielder hit a grounder up the middle that Chris Mahoney barely missed grabbing with his bare hand. The ball was headed right at second, which meant that it could have been Hutch's ball, or Darryl's.

Hutch let the shortstop take it.

Darryl flashed to his left, in front of the bag, and in that moment Hutch flashed right behind him.

Because he knew.

"Home!" Hank shouted from third.

Hutch knew the shortstop wasn't going home.

Darryl Williams gloved the ball and made no attempt to turn his body, or even glance at second, just shoveled the ball with his glove to where he knew Hutch would be.

Hutch didn't even bother with *his* glove hand, just barehanded Darryl's toss and in the same motion snapped off a throw to first that got the left fielder by two full steps and got the Cardinals the double play that got them out of the top of the sixth.

The crowd at Roger Dean made a sound that seemed to be a lot bigger than the number of people in the place.

Hutch smiled now, not because of the cheer, but because

Darryl hadn't even stopped running after he gloved the ball over to Hutch. He just slowed ever so slightly and nodded as Tripp took Hutch's throw and the ump at first made the out call, then kept running right into the Cardinals' dugout.

• • •

Hutch came up with two on in the bottom of the seventh. Alex had singled with two outs, a clean single up the middle, their first hit. Finally. Then Rocket Brown, still in there with a 2–1 lead, nobody warming up for Orlando, walked Brett.

Hutch had noticed something watching Rocket pitch to Alex and Brett: He was throwing fewer splitters now, just relying on heat more and more. Then he proceeded to throw four straight fastballs to Hutch. Hutch had missed two and two had been out of the zone.

Rocket wasn't just throwing fast now, he was *working* fast, and Hutch could see he was ready to throw the 2-2 pitch as soon as he got the ball back from his catcher, like he wanted to finish Hutch off *right now.*

So Hutch decided to slow things down a little.

He asked for time at 2-2, stepped out, rubbed some dirt on his hands, looked down at Mr. C in the first-base coach's box as he did, saw Mr. C make a motion as if *he* had a bat in his hands.

Then, right before he stepped back into the box, Hutch took a quick look into the stands. His dad was staring at the pitcher, but his mom smiled brilliantly at Hutch, like one more light in the stadium, and pointed to her head.

Telling him, in her own way, to dream a big dream for himself right here.

A big hit.

Rocket went into his stretch and came with high heat again. What the baseball announcers just loved to call high cheese.

Hutch swung right through the ball. Through it and underneath it and not even close to it. The ball was right in his grill and he'd been beaten by it, straight-up. Rocket Brown stopped and pointed at him before he ran off the field. "We're even now," he said.

Game 3 still wasn't.

Rubber Arm Mahoney walked the Astros' leadoff hitter to start the eighth, but when the next batter hit a slow roller in front of the plate, Brett was a blur getting to it and gunned the ball to Darryl covering second, and they cut off the lead runner. Chris took care of business from there, getting the next two guys to fly out.

It was still 2–1.

Six outs left. Nobody on the Cardinals was hanging his head. The dugout was as alive as it had been at the start of the night. There was all this chatter about how they were gonna do this, they were not losing this game, they were gonna get the first guy on and go from there.

The Rocket was out there again for the eighth. To Hutch, he didn't look tired, didn't even look like he'd broken much of a sweat even as he went deeper into the game. But Darryl hit the second pitch he saw for a double, then stole third. Hank Harding walked to give them first and third. But when Paul Garner struck out on an 0-2 pitch, Hutch was afraid that Darryl would stay at third with the tying run.

He didn't. Tripp singled hard up the middle, a clean hit. Even though he wasn't pitching, he and the Rocket were even now. The Rocket struck out Tommy O'Neill after that, threw a fastball at 0-2 that Hutch thought must have sounded like a police siren going past Tommy.

No matter.

Game 3 was 2-all.

Last ups, for everybody.

• • •

Taking grounders from Tripp while waiting for the top of the ninth to start, Hutch was calmer than he'd expected to be. There hadn't been a lot of conversation in the dugout as they'd all grabbed their gloves, other than everybody congratulating Tripp for his RBI hit. They were all business now, knowing the next play could decide everything.

So here they were.

Bunch of neighborhood kids, bunch of fourteen- and fifteen-year-olds from East Boynton and Boynton Beach and Lantana trying to be the best Legion team in the state. Trying to knock off the defending champs. Trying to do it at Roger Dean and do it on TV and do it in front of an even better audience than that—family and friends.

All that wrapped up in the next few minutes. It was another part of sports that Hutch knew he'd have a tough time explaining to people who'd never experienced anything like it.

Mostly it was the feeling that you wouldn't want to be anyplace else in the world.

A sense of being exactly where you belonged.

Pedro Mota pitched the top of the ninth. He had no problem with location tonight. He blew away the first two guys with fastballs, walked the next batter when he got a little too carried away with how hard he was throwing, then recovered to strike out Orlando's catcher on three pitches.

Just like that it was the bottom of the ninth.

Maybe the bottom of the whole season.

• • •

The Rocket came out, as expected, to pitch. Hutch was scheduled to bat fourth in the inning, which meant that he needed for somebody to get on if he was going to get one last shot at this pitcher.

His best friend was the one who obliged. Cody, who'd looked terrible all night against Rocket Brown, singled to lead off the inning from the nine hole. It was a good pitch, in on his hands, but somehow he managed to fist it over the first baseman's head and just inside the right-field line. It wasn't pretty. Didn't matter. Winning run aboard.

Alex fouled off a pitch trying to bunt. Then he laid off the second pitch he saw, thinking it was high, but the ump disagreed and said it was strike two. Which meant 0-2. Hutch looked down at Mr. C in the first-base coach's box, because even from over there he was the one giving the signs.

Mr. C kept the bunt on, even with two strikes. And Alex delivered for him, between the pitcher's mound and first. The Rocket got over to the ball quickly enough, took a look at second, then decided to take the sure out at first. One down.

But Cody was on second now, which meant a hit would win the championship.

Brett was up now, with Hutch on deck. Rocket got ahead 0-2 before wasting a high one that Brett laid off. Then Brett guessed right on the 1-2 pitch and ripped a fastball over third base, but he'd opened up just a split second early and the ball landed foul by a foot.

Hutch could hear everybody in the Cardinal dugout groan at the same time, like they'd all been punched in the gut. Still 1-2. Not for long. Now Hutch watched along with everybody else in the ballpark as Rocket poured a fastball past Brett for strike three. A fastball at the knees, on the outside corner, totally unhittable.

Dirty.

Hutch's turn. He put his bat down for a second, got some dirt to rub on his hands, saw that his hands were shaking. He told himself it was all right, these were *good* nerves, that he wasn't scared, that his whole life he'd wanted to be up in situations like this. A dream situation, with everything on the line.

Dream big.

Darryl came out of the dugout behind him. "Captain," he said.

Hutch turned around.

Darryl said, "You know how I'm always sayin' it's you or me in situations like this?"

"Yeah, D, I do."

"Don't feel like you have to wait on me tonight."

Hutch walked slowly to the plate, making himself breathe

deeply, trying to get his emotions under control, trying to get his mind just right, ready to stand in there against a pitcher who might just have thrown the best fastball he'd thrown all day. In the bottom of the ninth.

Hutch leaned over, rubbed more dirt on his hands, dug in now, looked out at the Rocket. Rocket checked Cody at second to keep him close, not about to make the same mistake twice in the game and let Cody just stroll over to third. Then he reared back and threw a fastball in the direction of Hutch's eyes. Threw one up and in and put him on his back, Hutch flipping himself backward like one of those backward high jumpers in the Olympics.

His helmet went flying. So did his bat, and the back of his head hit the ground hard. Even as he landed on his back, he was hoping the ball might have gotten away from their catcher so that Cody could move to third, but when he sat up, he saw Cody still standing on second base.

"Sorry," the pitcher yelled in to Hutch, even though he didn't sound very sorry. "Sucker slipped."

Hutch didn't think so. He was sure he'd been buzzed on purpose, sure that Rocket didn't want Hutch hanging over the plate for the rest of this at-bat. Hutch was just as sure of something else: The next fastball was going to be the one Brett had just struck out on, a fastball away. That was why Rocket had just tried to move him away from the plate.

Hutch didn't care where, but he knew he was hitting this next pitch hard somewhere. This wasn't like practice that time when his dad was watching and Hutch had nearly screwed himself into the ground trying to hit a home run, and ended up barely getting his bat on the ball. He didn't need a home run and neither did his team.

Just a base hit.

He'd never been more determined in his life to get one.

Hutch thought: This guy is *mine.*

He cleaned off the front of his jersey, started to get into the box, good to go.

It was then that he stopped. Like there was a voice inside his head telling him to pause.

The voice was his dad's.

"Hey," his dad would say when he wanted to get Hutch's attention, or even reprimand him sometimes. *"Hey,"* he'd say in a real sharp voice.

Hey, Hutch heard now.

He looked up to where his dad and mom were, and the Hesters, and Darryl's mom.

Looked there just as his dad stood up.

His dad was looking right at him.

Carl Hutchinson tried to make it look casual to the people around him, like he was getting up to stretch, not having to worry about blocking anybody's view because there was nobody sitting behind him.

His eyes, though, never left Hutch's.

All those nights and all those games when Hutch just assumed his dad wanted to be somewhere else. Not now. He was staring as hard at Hutch as Hutch had stared at him last night in the batting cage at Fallon.

Like he needed to get his attention.

Then Hutch saw why. Saw his father drop his hands the way coaches did when they were telling you to bunt.

Bunt?

Was he nuts?

His dad wanted him to bunt with the winning run standing there on second base? With two outs? And a chance to end this game with one swing?

Hutch said to the ump, "I need one more second, sir, I've still got some dirt in my eye." He stepped back, rubbed a finger in an eye that didn't need rubbing, then squinted over toward third base, as if he wanted to make sure he could see straight.

The third baseman was playing way back. Too far back and guarding the line, even though any kind of hit was going to win the championship for the Cardinals, whether it went for extra bases or not.

But still . . . a bunt?

Hutch put his back foot into the batter's box and dug in, and as he did, he shot one last quick look at his dad as he cocked his bat. Saw him nod again.

Then Carl Hutchinson did something he hardly ever did.

He smiled.

The Rocket checked Cody and then threw his fastball on the outside of the plate, just as Hutch had known he would.

Hutch bunted.

He dropped the bat head the way you did when you were bunting for a base hit, got the fat part of it on the ball, deadened the ball right down the third-base line, and took off for first.

Cody would tell him later that the third baseman started in when he realized what was happening, then stopped like he'd forgotten there were two outs, stopped like he thought he might have to cover third with Cody coming hard from second. Once he did, it was all over. He couldn't get to the ball in time, the Rocket had no chance, and neither did the catcher.

Hutch didn't turn around until he'd crossed first base safely. He wanted to clap his hands when he saw that everybody was safe, that they had first and third for Darryl. He didn't. Even now he was old school. He wasn't looking to show anybody up, not even the pitcher who'd just put him down.

He was just looking to win the game.

And he'd left it up to the team's best hitter to do just that.

Hutch did allow himself another look up into the stands. His dad was seated again, staring in at home plate.

But still smiling.

Carl Hutchinson wasn't in his seat for long. Nobody at Roger Dean was. Because on a 1-0 pitch, Darryl got everybody up. Because Darryl was the one making the scrapbook swing, putting that sweet swing of his on the ball, the ball making a sound coming off his bat that was louder than ever to Hutch, like something they could hear in the parking lot.

The ball cleared the Dunkin' Donuts sign with ease, cleared it and rolled toward the Cardinals' clubhouse.

Cardinals 5, Astros 2.

Championship.

All of the Cardinals were at home plate when Hutch got there. They started pounding on him the way they'd pounded on Cody and then they all waited for Darryl. Who was, of course, being Darryl, taking his time going around the bases, styling to the end.

When he got near home plate, he tossed his helmet away, the way David Ortiz of the Red Sox did when he hit a walk-off home run, and then it was the whole team there celebrating together, everybody pounding on everybody else, again.

Hutch and Darryl were the first ones to pull loose from the crowd. When they did, Darryl was grinning at him.

"What?" Hutch said.

Darryl said, "I gotta be honest, Captain. I would've been happy if it was you got the big hit." Now he wasn't just grinning, he was smiling all the way, as big as Hutch had ever seen from him. "But let's face it: It was *supposed* to be me."

Hutch laughed. "When you put it that way, I suppose it was."

Darryl said, "Ask you something, before I go talk to TV?"

"Anything."

"What made you lay it down like that?"

Hutch said, "My dad told me to."

"Told you," Darryl said. "Man can coach."

Then D-Will walked over to where the young guy from Sun Sports was waiting for him, walked in front of the camera and into the TV lights, as if that was another place where he was supposed to be.

And in that moment, away from the lights, away from the rest of the Cardinals, it was just Hutch and Cody on the big field.

"You know what tonight is?" Cody said.

"What's tonight?" Hutch said.

"The first of many just like it, dude. First of many."

Cody kept talking then, the way he did, but now Hutch wasn't hearing him, he was hearing Darryl in the clubhouse before the game, telling him that maybe everything he needed wasn't at some school up north, or anywhere else in this world, maybe it was right here.

Then Hutch left Cody Hester standing there and made

his way through his teammates, made his way through the gate at the end of the dugout and up through the stands at Roger Dean and did something he had not done in a very long time:

Hutch hugged his father.

And his father hugged him back.

ABOUT THE AUTHOR

Mike Lupica, over the span of his successful career as a sports columnist, has proven that he can write for sports fans of all ages and stripes. And as the author of multiple hit books for young readers, including *Heat, Travel Team, Summer Ball,* and *Miracle on 49th Street,* Mr. Lupica has carved out a niche as the sporting world's finest storyteller.

Mr. Lupica, whose column for New York's *Daily News* is syndicated nationally, lives in Connecticut with his wife and their four children. He can be seen weekly on ESPN's *The Sports Reporters*.